Life As We Knew It

Book 1 of
Transformation Project

Lela Markham

Breakwater Harbor Books, Inc.
Scott J. Toney and Cara Goldthorpe, Co-
Founders www.breakwaterharborbooks.com

Lauri Sliney
Aurora Watcher Publications
500 Ketchikan Avenue
Fairbanks, Alaska 99701
lelamarkham@gmail.com

A Word from Lela Markham

Thank you for reading my book. If you enjoy it, please take a moment to leave me a review at your favorite retailer. I appreciate it!

There are all sorts of reasons to write a series like the Transformation Project, but the main one is ... I still can. We live in perilous times in 2015 and for those of us who have studied economics, history and political science, the dark clouds on the horizon look ominous. As debt grows and military adventuresome increases, events could fundamentally transform America and forever alter life as we know it. Thinking that it cannot happen makes it more likely that it will happen.

References to the Roman Empire are quite common in the United States today because the comparison is appropriate. Many of the same stresses that destroyed the Roman Empire are pulling on the US today. In the waning days of the Empire, elections were costly, and funds were raised from questionable sources, creating the appearance (and probably the reality) of politicians beholden to special interests. Politics in Rome were a means to personal wealth for the politicians and their entourage. Rome was in a state of almost continuous war in the last decades of its existence. The Republic's leaders received a lot of money and attention by foreign powers. Profits made overseas shaped the Republic's internal policies. Rome's middle class was wiped out by the importation of cheap foreign slave labor.

Can we deny that these forces are not at work in the United States in the 21st century? Some of the specifics vary, but the dynamics are strikingly similar.

I took my inspiration from current events, from the frightening slide into mega-debt during Barack Obama's first term, from the revelation of NSA spying on American citizens, and from what I see as serious problems with presidential politics in the 21st century, then I brought them to a small town to humanize the story. Ultimately, this is a story about community with a backdrop of nuclear fallout and political intrigue.

During this first book in the series, you might have noticed that I pay inordinate attention to life as it is now – comfortable, prosperous, connected by technology and mobile. By the end of the series, I hope to show you just how fragile life as we know it is. The Roman Empire didn't transform in the era of bread and circuses, but the seeds were sown for that eventual collapse long before the barbarians started banging on the gate.

From this comes The Transformation Project, of which *Life as We Knew It* is Book 1. It is a look at the possibilities of the future given the circumstances of the present.

Lela Markham

Thanks!

To my parents for raising me in Alaska in a house built of books. What else was there to do but make up stories? What a wonderful environment to create a writer!

To my fellow Breakwater Harbor Books authors for their mutual support and, especially Ivan Amberlake as beta reader and editor of Life As We Knew It.

To President Barack Obama and First Lady Michelle Obama for making me consider what it would actually take to fundamentally transform America. I don't think this was what they had in mind.

To my Lord and Savior Jesus Christ for the innumerable blessings You gift to me each day.

Romans 5:3-5

Table of Contents

"It's not the end of the world at all," he said. "It's only the end for us."

Nevil Shute, On the Beach

Life As We Knew It

Book 1

Transformation Project

Kingdom Come

San Diego

She stood before the safe, one hand beckoning, the other holding the cloth-wrapped bundle. Her face hid behind the veil, but her large dark eyes were sad and angry. Shane slid up the wall, bracing himself in the corner, scrubbing tears from his stinging eyes with the heels of his hands. Time had come.

It had been years since he'd thought about God, let alone prayed. His heart had been certain that there was no god. Yet a verse floated up from some long-forgotten Sunday School.

... your kingdom come, your will be done, on earth as it is in heaven.

"This is my kingdom come," Shane whispered. "What I earned on earth and in heaven."

Her eyes demanded his obedience and his legs complied. The locked safe was no deterrent as he knew the combination. Guns on the right, clips on the left. The 9mm felt light in his hand. *Unloaded!* He always unloaded when he came home from a trip. The clip slid easily home and the gun felt right. Heavy. *Final.*

She stood to his left as she had that night, clutching the bundle to her chest. Shane raised the

1

gun as if to fire at her, but then turned it, put the barrel up under his chin, deep in the curve of his jaw and pulled the trigger.

CLICK! The sound echoed through the room like a shot, but far quieter.

Not bang? Shane felt the blood coating his hands as he stared at the gun, bewildered why his life hadn't just ended. He hadn't primed the first round. Racking the slide, he heard the round slip into the chamber.

If you're going to do it, do it right! Don't risk flinching, blowing your face off and living.

He didn't recognize the voice, but the man had a point. If you're going to commit suicide, you don't want to live brain damaged. Shane stared at the barrel, tongue working at the thought of putting it in his mouth. Her eyes bored into his soul while blood stuck his fingers together. *She* wanted this.

"This is my kingdom come," Shane whispered again. *When you serve Satan, you reap the whirlwind.* He raised the gun and opened his mouth to receive the barrel. He hesitated a heartbeat as the taste of carbon and gun oil filled his senses. Every instinct said not to slip his finger into the trigger guard. *Do it!*

"*We are ... we are ... the youth of the nation! We are ... we are ... the youth of the nation!*"

The cell phone echoed out of the safe, the long unheard ring tone jarring Shane from head to toe. He flinched, dropped the gun, covered his head as he watched it drop. It hit the threadbare carpet, bounced then slid toward the bed.

Shane stared at the cell phone – a cheap LG that he hadn't touched, hadn't powered up, in years. After the despised ring tone cycled three times, the phone went silent. With shaking hands,

Shane picked it up. Jacob. A moment later the cell vibrated to say a text was coming through.

Shane stared at the message.

GPJ - I'm praying for you!

The screen went black, like you'd expect from a discharged cell. *What the hell?* Somewhere on the other side of the house, someone began banging on the front door. Shane looked down at his hands. The blood was gone. He stared around his bedroom, recognized it as his bedroom. Not Ramah. *She* was gone. She'd never been here. *I'm freaking losing my mind!*

The banging became more insistent. You could come back from Miristan, but you brought it with you. He swept up the gun and headed for the front door, demanding to know who it was disturbing the peace at three in the morning...

"Abri la puerto, hermano," Shane unbolted the door while calculating the odds of Mike appearing at his door now or of Grandpa Jacob calling him on a discharged cell now.

"Where have you been, *amigo*?" Mike entered without being asked, filling the space with his large, active presence. "You're not answering your phone, your email. BW is freaking out! What's going on, Ric?"

Shane's hand shook so hard the gun rattled against the wood as he set it on the coffee table before sinking onto the couch. Mike blathered on for some time. Tight friend that he was, he wouldn't have been Shane's first choice to share this with. Big, loud, and aggressive, Mike was not a deep thinker. But he was here, and Shane reached for the lifeline before it slipped away.

"I think I'm losing my mind." His teeth started chattering with adrenaline.

Mike paused in his Spanglish monologue to frown at him, perplexed. "What's that supposed to mean?"

"For starters, I had that in my mouth when you started banging on the door."

Mike stared at him for a long minute, looking like he didn't understand what Shane had just said, but when Shane reached for the gun, Mike picked it up, cleared the slide and thumbed the safety.

"Okay, man. We're just going to keep this away from you for a while. It's going to be okay."

She moved in the door of the bedroom, but Shane knew Mike's presence would keep her back and for now, he would live.

Life As We Know It

Emmaus Kansas

In the northwest corner of Kansas, corn fields amid a sea of prairie grass undulated toward the foothills of the Rockies, dotted here and there with small towns and crisscrossed with highways and roads. In late-August, the fields were in their final burst of growth before the harvest, still green with just a suggestion of amber.

Emmaus, Kansas, drowsed in the heat, embraced by two ridges that were among the most prominent bits of land for a hundred miles. Sheltering some five thousand souls, Emmaus had been blessed by water and geography. You couldn't grow corn reliably beyond the western ridge, meaning she was surrounded by farms. A salt mine occupied one end of Mission Ridge and deep in a box canyon, Jericho Springs still produced clear, clean, artesian water. The surrounding typography made the airfield south-west of town attractive for small aircraft. Many of the younger people in the town were telecommuters whose full-time jobs were in Wichita or even Chicago. Emmaus had a good school system, making it worth the once-a-week drive to assure a boss that you weren't playing video games on his time.

Jacob Delaney pulled into the driveway and eased the truck into neutral. The engine chugged slightly on shutdown. *Time to tune 'er up! Later!*

The driveway was deserted except for Jill's Tahoe. Jacob had waited for that. The house stood near the front of a long narrow Metis lot, with three live oak in the front. Painted red with white shutters and fronted by a broad white pillared porch, it stood two-and-a-half stories tall with a full basement beneath. Except for the two-story addition to one side that held the master bedroom over a study and the additional rear porch off the kitchen, the house had been built in 1887 when the Delaneys had moved from Jericho Springs with half the town. It had sheltered five generations of Delaneys. Jacob hoped it would shelter more.

Today, he had his doubts. The sun seemed to shine less brightly, and the air had a static taste to it like just before a tornado. The occasional wink of sunlight off the wind turbine blades from the edge of Shoenfeld's soybean field usually didn't bother him, but today the rhythmic flash annoyed. That anticipatory sense of doom brought him home in the middle of the workday. God felt farther away than He had yesterday, and Jacob felt the need to share the burden, to ask another voice to lift it toward heaven with him.

He let himself in the back door into the mud room that had been a back porch. The washer and dryer and the stairs to the basement greeted him. Two steps up, the kitchen with its black- and-white vinyl floors and mellow pine cabinets stood deserted. He stopped at the door to the dining room with its oak antique sideboard, china cabinet and table suitable for seating a small army. Jill had pulled the drapes open to let in the sun and now sat in a wash of golden sunlight, the freckles on her arms standing out in the field of her summer tan. She looked up from her laptop.

6

"Am I interrupting?" he asked. He idly thought that he missed the pale blue Vi had painted the dining room 50 years ago. It had been a deep pumpkin orange for more than a decade now. *Why do I care today? I miss you!*

"No, just doing my morning Bible study." She pushed the laptop back. "What's up?" "What makes you wonder?" he asked. He loved his daughter-in-law. *How did Rob make such an amazing choice?*

"You left here a half-hour ago saying you had a field to spray, but now you turn up after Rob leaves. That usually means you want to talk to me, not him. What's up?"

Normally, her insight would have made Jacob grin, but today his heart wasn't in it. Jacob pulled his cell phone out of the breast pocket of his cambric shirt.

"I still text Shane ... every Sunday night."

Jill's green eyes rounded. She looked young for her age. Despite the red dye in her hair, the only lines in her face were from smiling, even though she'd had reasons to cry.

"That's persistence. How long since you've heard from him?" "More than a year. You?"

"He replied – if you want to call it that – to my invitation to Keri's wedding. Something about being overseas and not able to make it. It felt like a lie. That was six months ago. He goes through cycles. This one has been a dry one. Before that, I hadn't heard from him for nearly a year. I gave up the monthly email updates a few years ago."

Jacob nodded. His sons had done the same to Vi when they were gone to war, but they'd become so used to instant communication since the Internet. Non-reply was hard to take.

"So, he's always been terse in his texts, but ... the last two years ... it's like he's been replaced with

7

a machine." Jill nodded slightly in agreement. "Until last night, that is."

"Last night? Why'd you change your pattern?" It was Wednesday.

"Because I woke up in the middle of the night knowing he was in trouble. God said 'pray' and I did and then I texted him." He fumbled with his phone before handing it to her.

She saw Jacob's text.

GPJ - I'm praying for you!

Shane's reply came in this morning.

SHANE - I think God heard you! Really!!

"What does that mean?"

"I don't know," Jacob admitted. "Anytime Shane acknowledges that God exists, I find it hard to ignore." Jill looked at the third and final text in the train. Jacob had replied:

GPJ - Good!

"He didn't reply," she noted, handing the cell back to him.

"One message is more than I've had for a year and the timing .... I want to pray with you. Something's up with him. Maybe something that will move him in the direction he should go."

"Jacob, we've all tried to get him to come home ...."

"This is not the home he needs to come to, Jill. You know that!"

Jacob had liked Jill from the moment he'd met her more than four decades ago. She was a strong woman, even back when she'd been a girl. Jill didn't always agree with Jacob, but she took instruction well. He saw his comment sting her, but she also knew he was right. The home Shane needed to come to was not a physical one.

"I love you, Jacob," she told him. "Yes, we should pray for Shane together as we have prayed for him separately for so long."

Her hand brushed the laptop.

"Don't email him, Jill," Jacob told her. "Let God do the reaching."

A single tear spilled down Jill's cheek. She nodded and then pushed the laptop away and held out a hand to Jacob. It seemed so small and soft in his big calloused one.

They spent over an hour, hunched over the dining room table, praying softly – sometimes lapsing into silence. Once Jill had opened the laptop to find a Bible verse. Jacob preferred the Bible that lived in his head. They both wept for Shane and rejoiced that God knew exactly where he was. When they finally said "Amen", the sun was well toward noon. Jacob offered his handkerchief for her to fix her mascara.

"No, I'll take care of it upstairs. You know, Rob thinks he's doing something illegal."

"Could be. I hooked him up with Fess Stephenson's boy out in California before I knew he was running guns and whatever to Bolivia. But he didn't take that job, so .... I think he's working with one of those mercenary outfits, but that's more gut feeling than sure thought."

"Is that any better than doing something illegal?"

"They don't put you in jail for it ... usually."

Jill heaved a sigh and moved to gather her laptop. The motion brought the screen to life and she opened a new email. "Wow," she murmured.

"What? Way things are going today, is it Shane asking to come home?"

9

"No, that would be better, but ... Cai's in Wichita on business. He emailed 'Mom, have you heard from Shane lately? I just spent an hour on my motel room floor praying for him and I don't know why.'"

"Wow." Jacob shivered, and then reached for his cell in his breast pocket, read the text there. "Rob," he reported. "Same thing. Girl, if they're praying too .... Something's coming."

He saw goose-flesh rise on Jill's upper arms. She shivered. "What is it?" he asked.

"If it's something good, why do I feel so scared for him?"

Fear contracted Jacob's heart as he nodded. Fear for Shane and fear for ... something Jacob couldn't quantify. *Whatever's coming it will be life-changing.*

Foreshadowing

San Diego

Dylan Rigby stopped in the lobby of his apartment building to check his mail, wiping sweat from his hair. It was really too hot to run, but he thought he'd catch a short one before going to work. He'd cut it in half, because even early in the morning, the sun baked the streets. His mailbox held an envelope and some junk mail. He tossed the junk in the recycle can near the stairs and then frowned at the envelope. The handwriting seemed familiar. He trotted up the stairs to his 4th-floor apartment. When he looked at the envelope again while unlocking his door, he remembered seeing Alan Marquet in his cubical four days ago before he'd stepped in front of the cross-town bus. Dylan stopped by to ask him to coffee. Alan scowled at his computer screen, his dark brown eyes narrowed, his full lips pursed.

"Tax collector or psycho ex-girlfriend?" Dylan asked. Alan flinched and dumped the screen.

"You got me. Women!"

"Yeah! You want to go get some coffee? You can tell me all about it."

"Nothing to talk about." They went to coffee and talked about nothing, which was often how they

11

spent their breaks. Dylan remembered how distracted Alan had been. They'd gone back to work, separating at the elevator and Dylan had never seen him again.

Alerted by Alan's handwriting, Dylan glanced at the postmark. That same day. Anxiety clawed at his chest as he closed the door and tore the envelope open.

A thumb drive and a note slid out. Alan had pulled a thumb drive out of the computer before they'd gone to coffee.

> I don't know who else to send this to. I didn't know what it was when I opened it and now I'm scared. Maybe I'm panicked. If I'm still alive when you get this, we'll have a good laugh. If not ... maybe your dad ... I don't know. Maybe you should just destroy it. Just don't open it on a networked computer. Alan.

Dylan unplugged his laptop from the power source, disabled the wireless modem and entered airplane mode, then set it on the metal bookshelf that he'd designed as a partial Faraday cage. He then plugged in the thumb drive and opened the first folder on it.

Everyone in the services knew Marshall Ellerby, the head of Homeland Security. This document was a scan of a 1990 doctoral dissertation by Ellerby. As Dylan scanned through it, his throat grew tight and his stomach soured. It could be taken as a political science thesis on a multi-city nuclear attack from small-state actors or ... Alan had died for this. *Someone killed Alan over a freaking dissertation. Why ... unless it is important and active?*

He needed to tell someone, probably his dad, but ... but ... not now, not today. He'd learned in his training that the safety found in not attracting too much attention. He wrapped the thumb drive in a sandwich bag and buried it in the tin of coffee beans, and then he showered quickly and headed for work. Alan had panicked. He'd been acting strangely. Dylan knew acting like nothing was unusual was the best way to handle this -- and just hoped it was enough.

New York Package

New York City

The line at the Ferrara kiosk snaked toward the Merchant's Gate, which was what Bobby Noreen wanted. The busier the better. The lunch time crowd gathered at tables, along the sitting wall and at the base of the monument. Javier and he worked their dollies, headed through the Park to the Tavern. Bobby went in the side entrance to show his pass to the kitchen staff. A tall woman in a burgundy apron let them in the service entrance. The entire way, Javier Chavez wished someone would stop them and ask what they were doing, but of course, that would defeat the purpose of his mission.

"Stick in," his handler had said. "Until you can give us the network, there's no use bailing."

I can't let this happen. I won't. This is beyond the pale.

Bobby efficiently installed the refrigerant canisters and checked the gauges. Of course, the last canister in the row was not what it appeared to be. Javier could feel his cells breaking down just at the thought of what was safely contained in that shell.

15

Bobby handed off the clipboard to the manager, who signed the invoice. It seemed so above- board and ordinary. They walked back to the kiosk and got in line to get lunch, just two workers taking a break before their next delivery. Javier found it hard to joke with Bobby as they stood in line, got their food and ate it. He knew the importance of appearing ordinary and comfortable and Bobby sure seemed fine with eating so close to the destruction of a city, but Javier was not a mad man and he knew what they had just set in motion.

I won't do this. I must warn them. This cannot happen!

Still, he didn't lose a beat in the conversation and nobody who didn't know him would realize that he was freaked out. They finished their lunch and headed back toward the delivery van.

"Good job," Bobby said as they neared the van, wiping a sheen of sweat from his dark forehead, pulling off his cap to reveal his close-crossed black hair. Javier loaded the dollies, while Bobby hit the air conditioning. "Didn't even read nervousness off you, man."

"I'm pleased to do it," Javier said. "It's time this cesspool of a city was ended, for the good of all humanity."

"*Takbir,*" Bobby whispered.

"*Allahu akbar,*" Javier replied, smiling.

They drove for a ways, until they were far uptown.

"I need some cigs," Bobby announced and pulled over at a gas station. Javier waited in the van while Bobby ran in. As soon as Bobby disappeared inside, Javier picked up Bobby's phone, attached it to his with a pigtail and performed a quick download. By the time Bobby came out, the phone was back where he'd left it and Javier was smiling at the blue sky.

"What now?" Javier asked. "Do we stay in the city to be martyrs or are we traveling?" Bobby lit a cigarette and offered Javier one, which he turned down.

"I'll let you know as soon as I hear from the emir. Keep your phone on."

Javier nodded emphatically and rode in seeming peace to his apartment where Bobby let him out.

Will I meet the emir soon? Or are they just using us and this has all been folly?

Javier slid his mattress off the base so he could access the space beneath. The secure laptop powered up in moments and he began to scan what he'd gotten from Bobby's phone. In over a year of undercover investigation, he'd never had such a good chance to download Bobby's phone. He'd gotten bits and pieces before, but this time what flashed across his screen took his breath away. This was a lot bigger than just New York and if he read the plans right, Bobby knew of at least ten other cities that were at risk.

There were two people he needed to tell about what was happening and when. Grant Colby was first, routed through fifteen proxy servers to an email Javier hoped hadn't been compromised, to be delivered two weeks from now. The other was Jon Dracines, a New York Times reporter Javier had known in the Middle East, also routed through many servers and scheduled to hit his email September 25 at 6 p.m., leaving just enough time for him to report what he knew and save the city.

Insecurity

San Diego

A couple argued in sign language near the entrance. Shane kept his eyes averted so he wouldn't eavesdrop. Most Deaf didn't expect their conversations to be "overheard", but just like hearing the only Spanish conversation in a babble of English, it was hard to avoid reading sign when you were fluent...

Ouch, fella! Cheating's never a good idea!

Shane paused inside the door. He'd selected the old market because it wasn't large and should be quiet this time of night, but it echoed with the sounds of humanity. The overhead announced a cleanup on Aisle 4. Resigned to being uncomfortably close to people, Shane grabbed a cart and turned into the bakery section, shopping automatically, avoiding aisles with people in them, until he got to the milk, when he recognized the cooler seemed awfully barren. He set the quart of milk in the cart next to a loaf of bread, a box of cereal, a carton of butter. He stared down the aisle. His cart showed evidence -- butter because there'd been no margarine, corn bran because the choices were limited, luncheon meats too. Fresh produce looked empty and he bought designer toilet paper

19

for the first time in his life. He headed for the checkout line before the store went out of business.

Movement out of the corner of his eye caused him to flinch and reach for the gun he wasn't carrying. Mike wisely locked them up when Shane confessed his suicide attempt. Three teenagers laughed and shouted as they played keep-away with a roll of paper towels. *Maybe it's better I'm not carrying. I could be dangerous like this.* Movement at the end of the aisle drew his attention. A shadow of dark robes flitted at the corner of his vision.

"It's the trucker's strike," the guy ahead of him said to the checker. "It's supposed to be settled tomorrow." He gestured at his smart phone, where he must have the news up. The checker's expression said he knew that but didn't want to argue.

The kids made a racket, bringing Miristan alive in the supermarket. The building swirled around Shane as sound flooded over him. The overhead played some jazzy tune from a past generation too loudly. A dark-robed figure moved closer.

"... 57," the checker said. Shane stared at him. Middle-aged, a little paunchy. His hazel eyes narrowed as Shane stood frozen. "That'll be $15.57," he repeated. Shane glanced at the register readout and reached for his wallet. He felt naked without a gun in a back holster. He stared at the bills in his wallet. Normally, he'd have calculated the change by now, but his brain felt wrapped in cotton-wool. He handed the checker a twenty and decided to trust him to make correct change. The checker trusted the register readout.

Shane sat in the parking lot for 10 minutes, willing her to get out of the passenger seat.

He shouldn't have driven. He could have walked the six blocks. *Talk about distracted driving!* Finally, he started the car and prayed for no traffic. The working class neighborhood of post- World War 2 housing was quiet this time of night. Some kids played pickup as he passed the high school and a cab turned a corner a few blocks ahead. By the time he reached his small rented house, he anticipated another sleepless night. She was a shadow on the edge of his vision, but she would take solid shape when he tried to sleep, so he wouldn't.

Shane pulled up to the garage and looked up and down the street. A dog barked. The neighbor three houses down on the opposite side unloaded groceries from her trunk. Someone's flowers perfumed the air too strongly. The street lay quiet, and he thought he heard the whisper sound of drone blades a block over. A couple of blocks away, a car turned a corner.

Somehow it was harder to sleep when the neighborhood was quiet and yet Shane knew he'd be alert to every sound for blocks. It was the legacy of war. He'd never thought about what his dad must have gone through when he'd come back from Vietnam. *This? That would explain the drinking and the moving to a small town in the middle of nowhere.*

He actually breathed a sigh of relief to find Rigby sitting at his kitchen table; though his hand twitched toward the gun he didn't have before he recognized him.

"I guess I don't need to ask why you turned your phone off," Rigby said while Shane put the grocery bags on the counter. "When was the last time you slept?"

Shane shook his head. He'd lost track. The last time he'd lain down in bed, he'd tried to eat a gun when he woke up. Bedtime no longer seemed safe. He caught a few hours here and there, passed out on the couch. Drinking didn't seem to help the process, so he'd given it up as not worth the effort.

Rigby looked like a redneck tonight – plaid shirt, jeans, baseball cap. He appeared in Shane's life from time to time and you never knew who he might be – an accountant, a tourist, a cab driver .... *Soldier, tinker, tailor, spy.* He'd been Shane's handler for a half decade now.

"Whatever you want me to do ...." Was that his voice echoing through the house? *Why is the floor heaving up and down like a ship at sea? I should have taken out the garbage!*

"Don't worry about it." Rigby's gaze assessed him. "You clearly aren't up for anything right now. I knew you'd turned down a couple of offers from BW. When you turned off your phone, I got concerned. Glad to find you still breathing." He assessed Shane's reaction. "That bad, huh?"

"What do you mean?"

"Ramah still haunts you." Shane flinched, but Rigby didn't need to be told. It hadn't been a question. "You need to leave." Rigby sounded firm. "BW is not going to let a talent like Eric go easily and my asset Eric may have enemies. You should go back to being you."

Shane mulled Rigby's words over slowly.

"How do I do that?" He'd not given serious thought to that possibility for four years and now even casual consideration overwhelmed.

Rigby looked in his smart phone while Shane tried to remember how to think. "It's all doable. Give me a month to do some laundry. Do you want to go home straight to Emmaus or do you want to spend some time resting in Jericho Springs?"

Shane struggled to keep up. He'd bought most of the abandoned town four years ago under another assumed identity, back when Jacob convinced him he could go home again. He'd delayed for money and then *she* happened. He saw movement in the bedroom door. Rigby glanced over his own shoulder.

"She's not there. I searched the house thoroughly when I got here."

"What? Who?"

"You know what I'm talking about. You're seeing phantoms because of not sleeping." Shane shook his head in protest. *What happens in the bush stays in the bush. How does Rigby know?* Somehow he did. "You see her in your dreams, too. It's a Catch-22 – to sleep or not to sleep, either way you feel like you're going crazy." Shane stared at the government agent. "War definitely has side effects." Rigby sounded matter-of-fact. "Are you able to make these decisions for yourself?"

Shane remembered the taste of gun oil and slowly shook his head.

"Okay. I'm planning for you to go to Jericho Springs. I promise I won't do anything with your assets that Shane Delaney or his family wouldn't approve of. A month from today, you're headed there, and I don't want to hear any arguments."

Shane sighed. A 10-ton weight had been lifted from his chest. With the decision made for him, he just had to go with it. *You are not well. This is not you. It feels right!*

"Do I need to change the combination to your safe?" Rigby jerked his head toward the bedroom

"No, Mike already did."

"He's more perceptive than he looks, apparently. Good. Your grandfather -- can you call him or does a friend need to do that?" Shane stared at Rigby. *Am I thinking aloud? First Mike and now* …. "You're not the first asset I've seen hit the wall. It's especially not unexpected when coercion was used. I know you left a mess in Emmaus, but my intel says it's died down."

Shane flinched at Rigby's poor choice of words.

"Your grandfather has stuck in even when you studiously ignored him. I know your mom keeps trying too. And your friend Alex. You aren't alone unless you want to be."

There'd been a time when Shane would have objected to Rigby reading his emails, but reality was that government computers read everybody's email every day. That a human being read his wasn't news. Getting upset wouldn't change anything.

"They aren't going to like who I am now."

"No, but they'll love you just the same, Shane. Healthy families like yours do that."

Shane stared at the tabletop. *He's as wrong as Mike. I can't go home again.* Shouting filled his ears, the memory of angry words. He shook his head, trying to stop the sounds from the past, trying to negate what Rigby had said. And then that ridiculous ring tone filled the room.

"We are ... we are ... the youth of the nation."

Rigby glanced at the cell phone where it sat on the counter being charged. "Your private cell?"

Shane looked at the number.

"My grandfather gave it to me when I was leaving Emmaus. I guess he's kept the account paid."

"I'll leave if you want to talk to your grandpa."

"It's not him. It's my brother Cai." Shane let the phone finish ringing, setting it down.

"Ah! Do you hear from him often?"

"Not by phone. Occasional emails. And, you're right. He claims he forgave me." Rigby stared at Shane for a long moment, then stood up and laid a card on the table.

24

"Get ready to go home, Shane. If you need anything, have any questions while you wait, that's a secure cell where you can reach me without official oversight. Okay?"

Shane nodded. The phone buzzed as it received a text. Rigby retreated so quietly Shane scarcely noticed he'd gone. He picked up the phone and read the text.

CAI - Hey, Shane. You're on my mind a lot lately. I know you think I hate you, but I don't. Call sometime.

Slowly, tiredly, Shane texted a reply. He'd done this before, so many times with emails, but he'd never hit SEND. His thumb hovered over the button, then moved to the DELETE button.

Then, blowing out his cheeks, he hit SEND.

SHANE - I'm trying to believe that. Thanks for not giving up.

And with that, he opened the door to go home.

Community

Emmaus Kansas

Alex Lufgren walked slowly down the old farm road, amid scrub bushes interspersed with occasional live oak. A rabbit ran across the path. The gravel road had been so beat down that it no longer crunched under his boots. Alex wondered how long it had been since his father stopped farming this land. Longer than Alex had been alive. He rarely came down this way, except when people camped here. He'd seen their fire from the hayloft before the sun came up. He found them about where he'd expect to find them, camped by the old irrigation shed. The man fed small sticks into a low fire while the woman held a small child wrapped in a blanket, singing softly to her in Spanish. They'd pitched two tents and set up coolers around a neat camp with a beat-up truck and cab-over camper at one end. Somewhere off toward the creek, Alex heard a plastic bucket scrap gravel. He cleared his throat.

Their eyes widened as he stepped from the brush into the clearing. The man stood. Alex held his hands before him, palms out.

"Not looking for trouble. I own this land." They glanced at one another.

"We didn't see any trespass signs." The man's accent was Texan, maybe with a hint of Mexico in it.

"No. I'm not about having people arrested for parking on land I'm not actively using. I'm also not into being taken advantage of, so when I see someone out here, I come introduce myself, so they know it's not waste land."

The man nodded. He and the woman looked at each other again.

"We only planned to stay the night," he explained. "Our little girl is running a fever and we just--."

"Does she need a doctor?" Alex asked.

"No, she's just teething," the woman said.

"Okay. If she does, there's a clinic in town. I'm Alex Lufgren, by the way."

"Mark Ramirez." He shook hands with Alex's proffered right. "This is my wife, Alice, and our daughter Lisa. Our son went to get water from the creek. We'll pay for the campsite if you want."

"No, I'm not looking to get paid. I wouldn't trust the water from the creek, though. Lots of farms around here. There's a well around back. Let me show you."

Several doors accessed the shed, but Alex hadn't bothered to clear debris from any but the far one. He used the combination and showed Mark into the dim interior. The old pump works sat here out of the weather.

"You looking for work?" Alex muscled the big valve toward the open position.

"Yes." Mark was probably in his late 30s, a lean man with wiry muscles and dark hair that had no gray in it. "You know of anyone looking?"

"Me if you can show me valid ID."

Mark nodded, not surprised by the question. Orange water spilled into the trough. It had been a couple of years since Alex had tested the well.

"We both have Texas license, but no green cards because we were born here."

"Sounds good. I've got some odd jobs for the rest of the week and then my green field needs to be harvested. That's probably a week's work. About two weeks from now the combines will come through and I'll need workers then. So will my cousins and other folks around town. Most of it is contract work, so they won't ask."

"I appreciate you asking. I'm an American too."

Alex nodded. When the water flowed clear, Alex closed the smaller valve that diverted the flow over to a large sink against the wall. Orange water spurted over the worn enameled steel. Alex answered Mark's concerned expression with an amused one of his own.

"Come up to the house in the morning and I'll put you to work. How old is your boy?" "Fourteen."

"Might have some work for him too, but shouldn't he be in school?"

"Alice homeschools him, so we don't have to. Thank you for understanding, Mr. Lufgren."

"Alex. Lots of folks migrating through this time of year, following the harvests. How'd you find the shed?"

"Honestly, someone told me about it."

"Another migrant?"

"No, we're not really part of the community. They don't trust born Americans. There was a guy stopped on the Interstate with a flat tire last night. That was toward Denver. I stopped to help him. He seemed to know the area. I figured it was his land."

"You catch a name?"

"I don't want to cause trouble."

"No trouble. Clearly, I'm okay with this. I'm mostly curious."

"Jason."

"There's at least four in town, that I know of."

"This one was strapped."

"That would be Jason Breen," the tall blond farmer identified. "Yeah, he owns some of the land near the airfield." He gestured in that direction. "He would know about this clearing." Mark still looked concerned. "It's no trouble. My wife's sister-in-law is his daughter. Sort of an inbred town." That got a fleeting grin from Mark.

The water flowed clear. Alex shut off the water at the sink. He heard a pigeon coo up in the rafters.

"There you go. We'll leave the padlock here and you can use this screwdriver to keep the door closed when you're not using it.

"You know anyone looking for more permanent workers?"

"Might. I'll need to think about it. What do you do besides pick vegetables?"

"I work on cars and all sorts of machinery. Alice is a secretary, but she's waited tables, cashiered."

"Let me think about it and see what I can come up with. You got maybe two months of camping here before the weather starts to turn."

"I know." Mark gave him an odd look. "That's why we're hoping to secure permanent work, so we can afford a place."

"You're not headed back to Texas then?"

"No, I don't think so." Mark's tone remained friendly with a dismissive undertone. "I really appreciate this, Mr ... Alex. Did you really just offer to let us stay the season?"

"Yeah. I don't mind helping when I can."

Alice had taken the little girl into the camper when Alex returned to the camp. A boy with his parents' dark hair filled a pot with creek water.

"Like I said, you can use it for washing, but I wouldn't drink it or wash dishes with it. It's not just manure. It's fertilizer and pesticides. And the creek comes out of Mission Ridge, which had a lot of mines on it back in the day."

"We'll use the well," Mark assured him. "Maybe Pete could pay our rent by helping with chores around the farm?"

"It's not necessary, but if it makes you feel better ... this shed could use a good cleaning, if Pete doesn't mind. I'm Alex by the way."

"Nice to meet you," the boy said. "Dad says clean, I clean."

"That's what he says when you're here, anyway." Mark cast an affectionate smile at his son.

"Yeah, my dad said that about me too. I'd better get back to work." Alex walked on down the old farm road toward the county road.

Lord, thank you for allowing me to serve You in this way, he prayed as he walked. The big red barn and the yellow farmhouse were in view as he crossed the road. Mocha the chocolate lab dashed up, tongue lolling in the heat. Alex loved moments like this, seeing the fields stretched out to both sides, hearing the cows lowing in the pasture. He spied one of the nanny goats frolicking down by the fence where the county road was.

His cell buzzed in his jeans pocket.

KERI - Dinner at the folks tonight. 7.

ALEX - Do we bring anything?

KERI - Poppy.

ALEX - I LOVE YOU!!!!

Times like this Alex sometimes wondered how he could have grown up with Keri Delaney and not known she was his soul mate until two years ago. *Was it just because she's Shane's sister? That could have something to do with it? What sane man,*

*knowing Shane's temper, would fool with his little
sister?*

Shane came to Alex's mind a lot lately. Maybe
Keri's presence triggered the memories, but Alex
didn't believe in coincidence.

Shane's long absence disconnected Keri from
him in Alex's mind. Something else at work -- a God
thing. Alex turned into the barn where he'd been
servicing a tractor. While he worked, he prayed.
Mostly, it involved keeping Shane's image in his
mind, because -- truth be told -- Alex had no idea
what was going on in Shane's life that required
prayer. It didn't matter. God said pray and Alex
complied.

After a while, though, his mind wandered back
to the Ramirez family. Some people would say Alex
trusted too easily but he thought he liked Mark.
That might be a God thing too.

Sometimes people had good reasons for setting
out in the family camper to pick vegetables. Alex
hadn't heard that Texas was having economic
problems, but that didn't mean much. Maybe Mark
and Alice had other reasons. That wouldn't make
them bad people.

When his mind wandered too far afield, Alex
turned on the radio on the workbench. The local
station had a talk radio segment where people from
all over the county called in with their opinions. It
was mostly conservatives, but today some bleeding
heart called in to challenge the whole idea of profit.
Alex didn't consider himself a businessman, really,
but as a farmer, he understood profit and loss. Any
year when he made less than it cost him to bring
his harvest to market was not a good year. He
figured other businesses had the same
consideration. When he had surplus, he used it to
replace worn out equipment or repair the roof. Fact

was he relied on subsidies that paid him not to plant that lower 40 to keep his bottom line black instead of red. He sometimes questioned the wisdom of restricting production, but the subsidies could be relied upon and the crops might fail.

You really are wandering far afield, my friend. What about Shane? What about Mark and his family?

Alex turned the station to a national Christian outfit and let the music take him to a more restful and worshipful place while his hands went about the business of a farmer.

San Diego Package

San Diego

Phillip Marston stopped on the down-ramp of the Sawyer Energy building in downtown San Diego and presented his pass and work order. The guard looked it over and muttered into his radio. Phillip took his hat off and rubbed a hand through his sandy-blond hair.

"Hot one today," he said to the guard.

"Yeah and there's no air conditioning out here. Not that we don't like your service, but when's Brad coming back?"

Brad had been run over by a car last month to assure Phillip this route. Phillip doubted very much if Brad would ever be able to speak again, much less drive a van on a route, but for the purposes of the op, he told the guard, Driscoll, that Brad was in a body cast.

"Maybe next month. Depends how the physical therapy goes."

"Well, everything's in order. I've cleared you to the cafeteria too, while you're here."

"Thanks, man. Appreciate it."

Phillip pulled into the cool parking garage of the multi-story office building. He wondered how much carbon it took every day just to keep this place so pleasantly cool. Well, he was doing something about that, something that would bring down the entire building and the company with it, plus make a statement that people were not going to take corporations wasting the people's resources anymore.

He thought putting the explosives in refrigeration containers was really a brilliant idea to. Swapped out only once a month, building staff had no reason to look at them and, even if they did, the one canister didn't look any different from the others. He lined them up as he swapped out each used canister for a new canister.

One of these is not like the other.

When he was done, he closed up the cooler room, checked the neatness of his hair in the rear-view and rode the elevator to the third floor cafeteria, where he spoke pleasantly with a couple of secretaries and a food tech, ate his lunch, and then rode the elevator back to the garage to get in his truck and finish his route.

As he drove, he listened to the radio about the protests in the Core District blocking the trolley lines, focused on the greed of corporations. The City Police clashed with homeless in East Village last night. In New York City, two cops had been shot on routine patrol and Brooklyn rioted over the arrest of the shooter. What more evidence did he need to prove that the corporations were sucking the life out of the country and they needed to be stopped? Bringing down a building would get everyone's attention.

When he got home that night, he pulled out the cell he kept hidden in a cooling vent and texted:

DONE

Putting the phone back in its hiding place, he went to take a nice long shower as a reward for a job well done.

Not Safe for Democracy

San Diego

Grant Rigby liked to think that he did what he did because he helped keep the world safe for his children. That helped him sleep when an asset burned out, when he heard about a war somewhere that he helped start, when he watched the evening news and saw the death and carnage his war resulted in. There'd been no 911 since that day and the Boston Bombing had been the result of a failure by ICE, not CSA. In fact, CSA warned of possible immigrant terrorism years before. Jostin on the third floor worked that angle, trying to find young immigrants who would step out of line for their faith or politics or a girl.

Some days, though, Grant knew he failed and when Chavez' email landed in a secure box he kept for Chavez to contact him, he knew it. Chavez had been undercover for so long, it felt like the man had gone native. Nearly four years since the mission he'd done with Shane Delaney that had ascertained the kid had a facility for languages and the nerves of steel that would allow him to be a good operative. Chavez had come home, played the part of a burned out mercenary injuring someone in a bar fight so he could go to jail for eighteen months. There, he contacted the Neharis network, which all the intelligence said was a terrorist outfit headed for a big statement. Other operatives worked on other angles and felt certain something huge was going down. Chavez last contacted Grant six months ago saying whatever they were working toward would happen this year.

When Grant opened the email, he expected a short synopsis, some photographs, maybe some hastily copied documents. Instead, he found detailed plans for making bombs and not just any bombs, but suitcase nukes that could fit inside refrigeration canisters.

As he paged through the material, he realized that this wasn't just one city, but dozens, including San Diego. The last page caused him to stop breathing for long enough to feel dizzy. It was a grainy satellite photograph taken of Grant's boss, Neil Pervis, having drinks with the head of Homeland Security, Marshall Ellerby. Chavez made a statement at the end.

I don't think we can stop this. If you take it up the chain, Pervis will know and we're dead. If you take it over his head, you've no way of knowing who has been compromised. It's insidious.

The cell structure of this network makes it impossible to find the head of the hydra. Whoever they are, they've been very clever. Green groups, Islamic extremists, haters of corporations, rightwing militias -- they're not just targeting one group, but targeting many, playing on their anger at multiple things to create a revolution. And, I don't think we can stop it. I'm running to ground. I hope you do the same. If there's any way you can save this evidence for later -- I don't know. I'll be in touch P3 when it's safe. Goodbye.

Grant wiped sweat off his forehead. How could this be happening? And what to do about it?

Chavez was right. They could only trust themselves.

He whistled as he walked down the busy CSA corridor, took the elevator to the ground floor, and exited the building. On the four-block stroll through midtown, he considered who to contact first. By the time he got far enough away from CSA headquarters, he worked it out. *Emily is central, but her fears must to be addressed before I approach her.* He started with his father-in-law.

"Jim, it's Grant."

"I didn't recognize the number."

"No, this is a cell I use only for these types of calls. If I told you that the world is ending Wednesday evening and I want you and Ann to go with me, Emily and the kids to a safe location, what would you say?"

Grant's heart slowly crawled into his mouth during the ensuing pause. He counted on Jim's service in Vietnam to make him see the sense in this, but now he feared.

"I'd say what should we pack?" Jim finally answered.

"You believe me?"

"I've objected to your skullduggery and obfuscation, but when you're straight with me, you're straight and I think this is one of those times."

"Bring whatever is precious to you, what you can't live without. Expect to be unable to resupply for a year. I've got the food and shelter taken care of. And it's a continental climate -- hot in the summer, cold in the winter."

"When do we leave?"

"Tuesday morning." "What should I tell Mads?"

"That's up to you, but if this gets out, we're all of us dead. This has to look like a family vacation."

"Will do."

Grant hung up and texted Dylan. In some ways, this was the riskier phone call because there existed a possibility that Dylan was more loyal to CSA than to his own family. That sometimes happened with the younger operatives during training. But Dylan had taken the burner cell Grant had given him for these situations, so Grant still hoped the risk was small. A mother's heart must be considered above all else.

GRANT - Call me back from a secure location.

Grant leaned against the wall in a hotel bathroom stall and watched on the tablet as Dylan got up to leave his cubicle. Using the ubiquitous cameras, Grant tracked him to the street where he ordered a coffee, then sat down on a bench to call.

"What's up?" Dylan asked. The surveillance camera Grant had hijacked wasn't designed for long-range, so he struggled to bring Dylan's face into focus.

"The world ends on Wednesday at sunset. I'd like you to come with us to safety."

Stunned silence! He hadn't had time to pick up a bot and the tablet said he was clean, but Grant still sweated. As he gave Dylan time to think, he prayed to the universe that he was not wrong about his son.

"The frequencies have low-level chatter that something is happening Wednesday at sunset," Dylan said. "BW is calling up its forces to deal with it so we don't have to put the National Guard out on the streets."

"Yup, but I have a definitive threat. Everything you're looking at right now -- poof." Dylan shifted on the bench, eyes scanning the buildings in front of him.

"And you're not doing anything to stop it?"

"It's complicated. Best not to discuss here."

Grant watched Dylan decide, moments multiplying into seconds.

"Okay. When and where?" Oh, thank God!

"Bring only what's really important to you. We're leaving Tuesday morning at dawn."

"Thanks for trusting me, Dad. I know what you must have been thinking, but .... I'm not as enamored with this outfit as I thought I would be."

"We aren't keeping the world safe for democracy, that's for sure. I'll call with details when I have them."

"What should I tell work?"

"Nothing for now. The upper management is compromised."

"Alan Marquet gave me something before he stepped in front of that bus."

Grant hadn't expected that. His training warred with his gut and good old-fashioned common sense won.

"Don't investigate it but bring it with us. This isn't over. I just can't stop what's happening now."

"Got it."

They broke the connection. Grant watched as Dylan brought himself under control and then finished drinking his coffee before heading back to the office. Grant watched him all the way to his cubicle and then captured his emails. *He's gone back to work. He's with us. What a relief!*

Grant texted his wife on her cell.

GRANT - Call me on DL

41

Emily called him back on her burner cell. "What's going on?" she asked.

"Things are -- hairy right now. We need to go on an extended vacation. Discretely pack anything you want to keep in the motorhome and plan to homeschool the kids for at least a year."

"Seriously?"

"Yes. I've already talked with Jim and Dylan and they're coming with us, so please don't ask a lot of questions."

A long silence was followed by a heavy sigh. "Okay. I'll trust you."

"Good. We leave Tuesday at dawn. Expect that we're never coming back. And, there's food and shelter where we're going."

"Okay. You make it sound like the world is ending." When he didn't reply, she gasped. "Okay. I'll get us ready."

Grant hung up and looked at the zip drive in his hand. Chances were good that if he held onto it, he and his entire family would be dead by nightfall. Ideally, he would like to get the other information from Dylan, but if anyone suspected Dylan had it, he'd have died shortly after Alan, who died at least a month ago. No, he needed to find someone safe to keep this thumb drive, someone who unlikely to come up on the radar, who could also take care of himself if he did.

He opened a back door to Shane Delaney's cell and listened to a conversation he was having with Miguel Ramirez. Whatever Delaney saw in that loose cannon -- uh, human being and best friend -- when Grant got to his car, he texted Shane. They weren't really that far away, and he couldn't think of anyone better to fulfill this mission.

Storm Clouds

San Diego

They met at a corner bar in a working class neighborhood. Eric heard him out, rolling a beer stein between his two palms, contemplating the dark brew within as if it might have answers.

You couldn't call it fidgeting. If you didn't know Eric, you'd think it was just an idle gesture, but Mike recognized it as nervous energy.

"No," he finally said after Mike stopped talking. His green eyes hid behind dark lashes as he kept his gaze on the table and that slowly revolving stein.

"It's one last job and it's good money."

"Yeah. It's really good money for in-country. Too good. And, my lease is up. I'm packed. So, no."

"I told them you'd say that, *de paso*."

At the end of the bar, an old man lit a cigarette. The whole place smelled like a fifty-year-old never-cleaned ashtray. Mike supposed most of these men spent their lives on these barstools. Why else would they be here on a Friday morning at 10 a.m. *Wait! We're here, but we have jobs. Never mind.*

"I was hoping you were feeling better."

43

Eric's shoulders slanted. Mike waited. It didn't do any good to push him to answer. Mike never knew the definition of the word "oppositional" until he met Eric.

"I started feeling better when I made the decision that I was done. So, no."

"Yeah. I'll tell them, but they might not listen."

"Slavery's still illegal in the United States, Mike." He'd never stopped the slow revolution of the stein in his hands. Now he took a small sip of the dark beer. "They can't make me."

"No. They can just make you wish you'd said 'yes'." Eric shrugged. "So, this is it?"

"I leave Tuesday." Eric repeated what he'd said earlier in the conversation. "I'll call before I go."

"We could get together, tie one last one."

"Nah. I think that's not a really good idea for me. If you and Alicia want to get together for dinner, okay, but drinking .... I think I'll pass."

Mike took a deep swallow of his Dos Equis and nodded.

"Right. I forget you don't drink when the pressure's on. I should know that after all this time."

Eric seemed relaxed, except for his hands. Mike wished he knew what that was about. "So, this is Alicia's email. If you want to stay in touch." Mike handed him a strip of paper.

"I do," Eric said, securing it in his wallet. "This isn't me leaving you. This is me leaving the life."

"Right."

"You should think about it, too, *amigo.* Sooner or later, what we do, that ends in death."

"Or as emotional roadkill?"

"Something like that." Eric let a silence develop that was painful for Mike. "I am so grateful for your friendship, Mike. You have no idea how much it's meant to me."

"I feel the same. It's going to feel strange, not seeing you."

"BW will give up on me eventually and then I'll invite you out."

"You'll probably have a flight school."

"Don't know. I'm not where I can see that right now. What is this job that BW is willing to pay so well for?"

"I don't know, but they're activating a lot of us. They want me in New Mexico by Wednesday."

Eric set the stein down and looked at the display of his phone. He frowned. "I got something I gotta do. So, Alicia's *madre* lives in Santa Fe, right?"

"Yeah. I'm thinking about having her go there so we can meet."

"You've never met her? Man!" Eric shook his head, smiling at some private joke. "Yeah, you should do that."

"Maybe have her join me at the end of the tour--."

"No. Go Monday. You're an SOB when you get off a job. Let her meet the sane Mike before she gets to know you."

"Jerk," Mike teased.

"I'm right." Eric tossed some bills on the table, more than generous for the one, albeit imported, beer. "Text me if you want to get together for dinner. Make it tomorrow or Sunday, because I'm out of here first thing Tuesday morning."

"Sure. I'll talk to Alicia. You take care, man."

"You know it. One last thing?"

"Which is?"

"The movers come for the last of my stuff this afternoon. I'd like not to do a cross-country trip unarmed."

"You said you're feeling better?"

"I am."

"For sure?"

Eric looked Mike right in the eye.

"I swear I won't try to hurt myself ... at least not before I leave town."

"Not the most comforting assurance I ever heard."

"I never expected to have it come to that, so .... I can't make promises for longer than I can keep."

"When you get where you're going, you have family, right?"

"Yes."

"Then promise me you'll tell them if you start having those thoughts again."

"Sure. I promise."

Eric can be trusted to keep his promises. And if he doesn't? He will!

"Okay. It's your name, alpha-numeric."

"Seriously? That easy? I never would have figured that out."

"That was the point."

They stared at each other, awkward, for a long moment before embracing for the first time in their friendship, then Eric glanced at his phone again.

"Gotta rock. Call me."

The last Mike saw of him was his tall athletic form and dark curling hair going out the door.

Mike finished his beer and then texted Alicia.

MIKE - You want to go to NM, see your mom? Monday? Sunday? Dinner with Ric Sat?

Mike tossed down some bills atop Eric's and headed for his car.

New Mission

San Diego

S hane watched Mike as he headed for his car from the front window of a coffee shop across the street, loneliness pricking his heart. His momentary distraction served Rigby well as he slid into the seat across from him. This time he looked like a businessman with glasses and a power tie.

"How are you doing?"

"Better. Packing the last of my boxes seems to have helped."

"Don't confuse busy-ness with euthymia," Rigby responded. Shane grimaced. "I know I said you'd have no responsibility beyond packing, but something's come up."

Shane grew guarded. Rigby had always been more or less straight with him, but his first handler gave him every reason not to trust and that never wore off.

"What's that?"

Rigby pushed one of the two coffee cups toward Shane.

"What I'm giving you is vital. I don't need you to do anything more with it than put it in your safety deposit box when you get home. Someday, someone will come and ask for it. He'll say Chavez sent him or else it will be Chavez. Or it might be me. Be careful who you give it to. Chavez is the safe word, but you may actually know the face. Make sure none of us have a gun to our heads."

"Why? What is it?" Shane took a sip of the coffee and felt the thumb drive under his hand. *How does Rigby know that I drink red eye?*

"Now don't go asking uncomfortable questions at this juncture. You're out of here Tuesday morning?"

Yeah, but I'm not exactly free, am I?

"Maybe earlier. Once my stuff leaves today, I'm open."

"Make sure you are out of here by Tuesday morning. This conversation would usually involve you turning in your work phone and tablet, but I'm not deactivating Eric." He pushed a portfolio toward Shane, who surreptitiously slid the thumb drive into a pocket. "He leaves International for Los Angeles headed to Thailand Tuesday morning. Shane hits US soil in Las Vegas Tuesday night. Your car arrives at Fashion Valley this afternoon. Key and plate number are in the packet. Make sure you've headed out before the sun comes up Tuesday."

They'd done such car swaps before, but this time Rigby had "laundered" Shane's Jeep that he'd left parked in a storage unit when he'd gone to South America five years ago. It had been "sold" three times and currently belonged to Joel Rhys, the owner of Jericho Springs, one of Shane's alter-egos.

"Okay." Shane slid the portfolio into his inside pocket.

"I'm serious. No later than Tuesday morning. What are your travel plans?"

"Spend the night in Barstow, push onto Denver Wednesday, maybe spend the night --."

"No! Look at me, Shane!" He always called him Eric in public, so Shane fixed his gaze on Rigby's face. "You need to be in Emmaus or at least east of Denver by sundown Wednesday.

Don't be anywhere near any large cities. Got it!"

"Yeah. Something's up, isn't it? BW is activating huge numbers according to Mike."

"You know I can't tell you. Treat this as a job until you get through Denver and swap out your license plates. You gave good advice to Mike about his mother-in-law. Timing's good. This may well be the last time we speak for a long long time, so I want to say it's been a pleasure working with you."

"How do you know what I said to --?" Shane read Rigby's expression and shook his head. "There's no such thing as privacy anymore, is there?"

"Not in large cities, but maybe where your folks live. Some, anyway. Take care of yourself, Eric. When you get to where you're going, let it heal you."

"Uh, yeah, I don't think ... it's always been a place to take a break between adventures."

"Trust me. Life itself will be an adventure soon enough."

Rigby stood.

"Keep your wits about you," he advised and then he was gone. Shane shivered. *Damned air conditioning!* Taking the coffee, he headed for his truck.

Georgia Package

Atlanta

Spring Street lay quiet on Monday morning after the rush hour. Tuck Snowden expected more security screening to enter the Russell Courthouse, but the Bunnell & Wilson security guard thought he was dealing with another BW employee, so when Tuck's pass checked out, they did a cursory check for bombs under the van and waved him through. After all, he was just delivering air conditioning tanks.

As Tuck worked to swap out the tanks, he thought about the trial that would start tomorrow for the two terrorists who had tried to blow up the Galleria. The trial took more than two years to come about and Tuck didn't believe they'd be found guilty. The Arab community insisted this was a false arrest and prosecution. The jury would cave. It wouldn't matter though because the explosives would take down the entire building and assure that justice would be done. It was time these Arabs understood that they could not just run roughshod over the American people without some blowback. If he had his way, he would deport them all.

Only 36 hours and the statement would be made.

First Date

Emmaus

Poppy? Like the flower?" Pete thought she looked more like a sunflower with her blond hair and long limbs.

"I hate my name," Poppy typed into the smart phone, which produced a pleasant female voice in a slightly robotic cadence.

"Why? It's unusual. Do you know how many Pete's there are in the world? Tons. Poppy is rare."

"Really? I guess. There was a woman here -- Deaf woman -- who was important. My parents named me after her."

"I'm named after my grandfather -- Pedro, but they Americanized it."

"Who?"

"My parents. Mark and Alice."

"Very American names. Alex say you will help with chores."

"Yup. You show me."

"See the truck? Those bales hay and straw need to go into the mow."

"The what?"

"The mow." She stared at him while he tried and failed to define the word "Tour first."

When he'd finished cleaning the shed, Dad said to ask Alex for some chores. Pete thought it would be boring, back-breaking work, but then he'd realized he'd be working with tall, beautiful Poppy. The phone made her muteness a mere inconvenience and it gave them something to talk about. Pete liked computer gadgets and Poppy knew a lot about the voice-to-text app. They spent a good twenty minutes walking around the farm yard, her identifying items that might come up in conversation.

Pete hadn't wanted to get stuck in Kansas, but he knew his parents wanted to be and Poppy might make it bearable. Mom was interviewing for a job at the grocery store today. Maybe they would be staying.

"So, tell me to shut up if you want -- but how come you don't talk?"

Poppy grinned as she took gaffing hooks off the barn wall. He took them while she typed. "I'm deaf. I can talk, but I'm hard to understand because I can't hear myself ... or you."

"That's why you sign?" She nodded. "Cool. Could you teach me?"

She wiped her hair back from her forehead, her blue eyes crinkling at the corners. "It's a language, you know. I can't teach you in five minutes."

"I already speak Spanish and English. I think I can handle a third language." She rubbed her chin with the back of a hand.

"All right. We'll do it."

She began providing signs for new terms, though once they started working, they relied on pantomime because she couldn't type or sign with gloves on. Pete hadn't done a lot of the work she directed him in, but she was a good teacher, demonstrating how to winch the bales from the

54

truck up to the mow - the loft above the barn. She showed him how to use the gaffing hooks to grab the bales and drag them into the corners of the mow. After the hot sticky work of the barn, she offered to show him around the area and take him to a local swimming hole. She provided a pair of trunks and they took mountain bikes through a woodlot to an old dirt road that led to a pond.

Pete stared around at the bluff to the north and west, the shading trees, the water. "This is not what I thought Kansas would be." Pete tried to sign it.

"Flat as pancake, no trees," she typed. "More west, more flat, fewer trees. Dust belt."

"That was here?"

Poppy turned west and then pointed left.

"South I-70. Turn off phone now for swimming."

It wasn't as easy without the phone, but they managed to communicate basically. It never occurred to him that he could read lips, but when she mouthed words, he mostly understood her. After they cooled off, they dried off on the deck of a cabin on the shore.

"What is this place?"

"Delaneys live here before town moved for the railroad." She read his expression. "Went north of ridge, bypassed Jericho Springs, so moved town became Emmaus."

He looked around.

"Jericho -- for the walls?" Frowning, she stared around the valley before nodding and shrugging.

"I want to show you."

A copse of tress on the other side of the pond hid a ghost town. Most of the buildings had fallen in and a building that might have been a store leaned precipitously. A brick bank still stood with rusted bars at the windows, but holes in the roof. A building that announced itself as the Jericho Springs Hotel looked well repaired.

"Someone bought, repaired 3 or 4 years ago."

"Someone lives here?"

"No. Mysterious."

They crossed a bridge over a dry creek and climbed to a blue and white building right where the ridge curved around to the west.

"This is newer?"

"Well house. Maybe 40 years old." She scrambled up a ladder, so he followed her. On the roof, she gestured for him to turn around and look. The valley spread before them and he could see the windmill at the farm.

"Beautiful," he said.

Sunlight filtered through dust motes and the air scented with flowers he couldn't name. He pointed to a blue roof set apart from the rest of the town and signed a question.

"Sullivans."

"Who?"

"You don't know Sullivan?" He shook his head. "Rich, big company, all over world. Lived here long time. Used to live there. Built big house on Heights."

Even as they watched two trucks came down the road. One turned into the Sullivan place and the other pulled up behind the hotel.

"What is that?" Pete asked.

"Don't know. Looks like owners moving in. Sullivan sold that house long time ago." She looked up at the west ridge. "We should go back. Rain coming. Sundown soon."

The trucks were still at the two buildings, workers going in and out. When they got back to the farm, Keri asked for help unloading groceries, and Dad was there looking for Pete.

"I'll see you tomorrow," he signed slowly. "You ... uh, heck," he said aloud, "I don't know the rest, but you can teach me more honest labor."

"I would like that, Pete of the common name."

"Nice to spend the afternoon with you, lovely Miss Poppy." Yeah, living here in Emmaus would have its benefits.

Friends Forever

San Diego

Alicia stared at the eggplant dip on the pita Eric offered. "What's it called again?"

"*Baba ghanoush*," Eric repeated. "Give it a try. It's not spicy."

"I'm a Chicana, Eric! Spicy doesn't scare me."

She took the pita and popped it into her mouth. Eggplant was ... interesting. Eric laughed at her expression. His laughter sounded good because it had become a rare commodity in recent months.

"That's my girl," Mike encouraged. "This is the guy to teach you to like all sorts of foods. What did you order?"

"*Shish tawook*," Eric said. "I figured *mujaddara* is pretty mild, so I'd go spicy."

"And what did you order for me?" Alicia felt a bit alarmed as Eric popped an *aleppo* in his mouth and smiled instead of answering.

"Ric." Mike sounded testy, but his brown eyes twinkled.

"Just *couscous*. Try one of these, Alicia." Eric offer her a bow-tie shaped eggroll.

"What is it?"

"*Sambousa*. It's basically an eggroll made with ground mutton."

The different flavors weren't upsetting her stomach so far, for which she was glad. Breakfast hadn't been so fun this morning. She wanted to enjoy this last evening with Eric, who had always been a great friend to Mike and gentle with her.

So hard to believe that he is riding off into the sunset tomorrow morning.

"So, Mike says you won't give us an email address, but I wanted to give you mine so that you will get in touch with us when you have time."

She pushed the paper toward him. He looked at it and folded it into his jacket pocket.

"It's not you guys I'm trying to get away from." He looked sad, so unlike his usual fun sense of humor, laughing and joking. Since the last trip to Miristan, he'd changed so that Alicia both feared for Mike without Eric guarding his back and feared for Eric if he returned to guarding Mike's back. "But I can't risk BW hacking your email and figuring out how to track me down. After I've rested a while, I'll contact you – I promise."

It felt strange not to drink any of the wine, but she was proud when Mike handed over his keys without an argument.

"Come on, the designated driver can have half a glass," Eric insisted. "This a really good Lebanese vintage and he's going to end up on his ass if he drinks three-quarters of the bottle."

She glanced at Mike. He nodded and she pulled the trigger. "I can't. I'm pregnant."

"You're kidding?" He looked stunned for a second, then high fived with Mike and called him Popi. "So, how far along?"

"Two months. You are the first to know besides us two. We're telling my mom on this trip. So, you need to get back with us fairly soon, and tell us your real name because this kid's getting named after you." She'd kept her voice low. There'd been a time when he would have been flattered and found a way to tell them, but now a muscle bunched in his cheek and he couldn't meet their eyes.

"How do you know Eric is not my real name?"

"Because you don't answer to it when you've been drinking," Mike said. Eric chuckled.

"I was distracted that night and you know why."

"Yeah, and the guy who never gets drunk, did. Come on, Ric. You're leaving. What's the secret?"

"Let's keep this pleasant, Mike, please. Maybe when I'm away from here – but not now, not here. Besides Eric ... Erica ... both names would go well with whatever your real last name is." Now his green eyes twinkled for a moment. "Do you know your husband's real last name?"

"No."

"Then knowing mine is not that big of a deal. I've been Eric for a half-decade. And there's really no feminine for my real first name."

The entrees arrived then, and they changed the subject. After the stuffed figs and baklava with coffee, they moved out to the front walk. Eric and Shane shook hands and Shane leaned down to give Alicia a kiss. Both of them remembered the drunken kiss she'd given him one night two years ago when she'd turned too soon in the hallway of a bed-and-breakfast and slid into bed with him instead of Mike, but Eric had been honorable and he'd never mentioned it since. She felt his hand slide something into her side pocket. *Whatever he's giving me, he doesn't want Mike to know about ... yet.* She didn't acknowledge it.

"You guys take care. I love you. And, hey, I know you had a bit of wine tonight, but Mike, leave town first thing in the morning, okay?"

"I said I would. She might need to drive so I can sleep."

Then Shane turned toward his truck and they turned toward their car.

"I'm going to miss that guy." Mike's voice vibrated hoarsely.

"Me too. I'm sorry to do this, but I have to go to the bathroom before we head home."

"Yeah. I'll wait here. You should take the keys. Pretty sure I'm over the limit."

Inside the restaurant, she checked her pocket and found two cards. One read:

SHANE. You can tell Mike tomorrow. And leave town like you said. Humor me.

On the second card, Eric had written:

Joel.Rhys @hotmail.com. Don't tell Mike until I say.

She took a photo of both cards with her phone, shredded and flushed them, all the while wondering. *If he's Shane, who is Joel Rhys and why is Eric/Shane using his email?*

Sculpting Dragons

Emmaus

Nevada Randolph shut down her rosebud torch and pushed back her welding mask. The respirator made it tough to breathe, especially on hot evenings. It wouldn't be too much longer, and it would start cooling off at night so she could work the forge.

The dragon was finished, except for the gas valves. She could imagine it gracing the courtyard of the hotel in Chicago, occasionally blowing fire from its nostrils. She walked around it, looked at it from all angles, and then texted Drew Albright to tell him it was finished. Drew's friendship was incredibly important to her. His connections in the business world were artsy enough to benefit her and then there were the friend benefits. His husband would freak if he ever found out, she supposed, but you couldn't expect the man not to scratch his itches. Besides, she was as discreet as Drew, so Max need never know.

Kim came to the door of the shop.

"Hey, kiddo, what's up?"

"Done with my homework." Kim pulled her long honey braid over her shoulder. "Thought maybe I could borrow the car to go up and see James."

"It's after nine, honey. His mother objects when you go there so late on a school night."

"I know, but we're just going to walk for a while."

"You know my advice on this." She read Drew's return text.

DREW - Thursday is our anniversary. I'll meet you in Chicago tomorrow evening. We'll make an evening of it, have dinner. I'll need to be back here by Wednesday evening, so I've set an appointment with Lazaro in the morning.

"I've got an appointment in Chicago on Wednesday," Nevada told Kim. "You'll need to take the dance classes tomorrow and Wednesday."

"Okay. I guess I'll go take a shower instead and then call James. It's looking really pretty." She indicated the dragon.

"This is my best one so far."

"Good night."

"You too."

Outside the crickets chirruped and the air smelled of the nearing harvest. Nevada lit a cigarette and leaned against the porch railing thinking of the coming fall and the sale in Chicago that would allow her to not worry about money all winter. Across the field, she could hear the horses in their paddock. The landlord's horses, but Jill was teaching Kim to ride. It was a good deal here -- even if Drew only wanted to be a friend with benefits.

She put out the cigarette in a can of sand and turned to the house and her most precious item -- her beautiful daughter.

Wet Work

San Diego

Dylan Rigby watched the tablet as Eric Faraday left the restaurant and turned toward Fashion Valley mall. His decision to leave tonight rather than tomorrow made sense. It was simply easier to cover a night departure and to avoid drone detection. For whatever reason, Grant wanted Eric's trail covered. Dylan had only been an analyst for a year and he had no real field experience, but he was a fully trained operative. Still, he'd been surprised when Grant asked him to cover Eric's departure.

What do you know that I don't, Dad?

Dylan trusted his father. He'd seen too much in the last year not to believe that the world might end Wednesday evening. Alan hadn't stepped in front of a bus accidentally. He knew that. *Why is Eric Faraday important in all this? He's a burned out agent going home to heal, but he's something more to Dad because he authorized me to do whatever is necessary to see he gets free of San Diego.*

The blue truck pulled into the parking lot and slid into a spot two rows over. Dylan couldn't see him very well, but he could guess Eric was scrubbing the truck. He would have had it detailed over the weekend, just like he had a cleaning crew coming tomorrow to scrub the house. Deep-cover operatives performed this ritual every time they left one cover identity to go to another.

Dylan slid out of the car as Eric entered the mall. An operative with Eric's experience knew how to avoid most of the cameras, but it was hard to do these days, so he would seem to be shopping and of no interest before heading to the Jeep. Dylan, watching him from a distance, saw when he picked up the tail. Within thirty seconds, he could tell that Eric was aware. *He didn't pick me up. I guess I'm better than I thought.*

Eric did a crazy Ivan, heading back in the direction of his surveillance. The lone stalker couldn't call for backup after Eric passed him. B&W typically didn't commit more than one agent to a tail. The tail hung back farther to follow Eric while Dylan followed the tail. Eric turned into the bathroom corridor. Dylan closed the gap with the tail.

Public restrooms were, well, public, so someone else occupied a stall while Eric washed his hands. The tail, striving to look normal, entered a stall. Dylan, out of view of the mirrors and stalls in the entrance area, signaled Eric and held up his CSA badge. The citizen left the restroom. Eric leaned over like he was going to wash his face. The tail didn't move. Dylan sidled up beside Eric who quickly and silently stepped out of the room. Dylan went over to the hand dryer, taking his time. The BW agent came out, saw him, flashed a momentary expression of concern and then left the restroom. Dylan didn't follow immediately, but quickly located him in the mall looking for Eric. Following at a discreet distance, Dylan followed him outside. As the tail neared Eric's blue truck, Dylan saw him reach into his pocket for a cell phone.

Dad said do whatever was necessary to cover Eric's trail.

Taking a deep breath, Dylan slipped up behind the tail and pressed his gun into the guy's left kidney.

"Uh-huh. Let me see this." He took the cell and read the unsent text.

BW397 - Faraday got away from me. I think he's swapped rides. Are you sure this guy is just a pilot?

Dylan found the man's wallet in his rear pocket.

"Who do you work for?" The BW credentials pretty much told him.

"I'm just shopping, dude. What's your interest?"

Dylan felt his muscles bunch and saw the flash of the knife as he came around. Must have had it up his sleeve. Dylan caught his wrist and broke his grip. The knife skittered across the pavement. Dylan punched him in the throat, took him to the ground and choked him out. The BW agent knew that he was dead long before he stopped kicking.

The world is ending day after tomorrow. You may be the first man I kill, but I doubt you'll be the last.

When the agent breathed his last, Dylan thought about what to do with the body. Compromising Eric Faraday's truck was not a good idea. On the edge of the camera shadow, Dylan could conceivably drag the body to his car, claim his buddy had too much to drink if they encountered anyone. He decided to risk it. Halfway to his car, he passed a red truck with a tonneau cover. He undid the cover and boosted the body into it. With luck, nobody would find the body before morning when the truck was miles away from the mall. By then, he and the rest of the family would be headed out of town. He felt momentary regret for ruining someone's day tomorrow, but he had a job to do.

In his car, he checked the number the text had been directed to. Eric's B&W supervisor's number. Dylan texted Grant to get a back door for the supervisor's email, afraid to call lest his voice betray how shook up he was. He'd never killed anyone before, and it was scary how easy it had been.

Eric picked up surveillance because they wanted him for the nationwide op and they didn't want to take "no" for an answer. After watching the red truck drive away without looking in the bed, Dylan sent a new text as if he were the operative.

DYLAN AS BW397 - He got away from me, so I couldn't put the screws to him. Guy looks like a zombie. You sure you want me to bring him in?

A few minutes later, a return text came in.

BW32 - Myerson says he's a vital asset. Did you check his house?

DYLAN AS BW397 - Yes, but he's not there right now

BW32 - I guess go home but meet him at the airport in the morning.

DYLAN AS BW 397 - Will do.

Dylan used his own phone to text Grant's assistant, informing of the retrieval order on Eric. Then he drove on as calm as he could be. Until he got to his grandparents' place where he was spending the night, he didn't let himself think about what he had just done. He took a long, long shower, vomited twice and cried until the hot water tank ran cold. Then he went to bed and stared at the ceiling until dawn.

Smoke & Mirrors

San Diego

Grant Rigby worked for the Central Security Agency for more than 20 years and he ran a stable of assets as valuable to the agency as stallions among draft horses.

Consequently, Grant became privy to secrets few knew, and fewer still would survive. Project Sunset wasn't the first black flag operation orchestrated by affiliates of the American government he had been aware of before they occurred. Early in his career, he'd nearly been liquidated for objecting to an overseas bombing. Knowing he couldn't prevent this one, he naturally used his stable to even the odds of survival. Activating Shane Delaney had been a calculated choice, not an act of desperation.

That's what he told himself as he loaded his family into the motorhome and drove east across the Rockies toward what he hoped would be a new life, shrouding their path in smoke and blinding any seekers with mirrors.

When Shane Delaney became Eric Faraday, there'd been a lot of behind-the-scenes smoke-and-mirrors. Shane Delaney had supposedly been flying cargo planes filled with something questionable all over South America for the last five years. He sent money home to Farmers Bank in Emmaus regularly and his email routed through an IP address in Panama's thriving ex-pat community.

Shane Delaney proved easy to hide. Except for his family and an angry man or three in Kansas, nobody considered him all that important. Eric Faraday's disappearance would be noticed. He owned assets that would be useful to him in "retirement" and skills valuable to both of his employers. Bunnell and Wilson was not interested in letting those skills go. The largest wholesale food distributor in the world had fingers in many pots, not the least of which were the wars in the Middle East. Mercenaries were money and Eric Faraday was a multi-skilled agent and veteran of multiple tours. His decision to retire just before a major operation sent up red flags. His refusal to be swayed by a huge bonus turned a spotlight on his activity.

Of course, BW's subsidiary Knight Industries had no idea who Eric Faraday really was because Eric Faraday never existed prior to five years ago and he only existed to work for Knight or BW and collect information for a covert government operation. Rigby's employers weren't too happy to be losing Eric's skills either.

In his long career, Grant Rigby gained a reputation for building iron-clad cover personas. When he groomed an asset, he built a back door because he knew slavery was still unconstitutional and assets might eventually want to live real lives again. Unfortunately, Shane didn't come with a clean slate. He'd worked for the government before. It hadn't been his choice and it hadn't gone well, but he'd completed the assignment. That record made reinserting him back into his own life tricky.

Grant got him before he'd become Eric, though, so the back door was there. It just wasn't as clean as he liked.

To reverse engineer Eric back to Shane, Grant laundered financial assets, reissued passports as well as pilot and commercial truck licenses, and hacked computer databases to swap out DNA, fingerprints, and facial and iris recognition data. He "resurrected" Shane Delaney and brought him to the United States while "retiring" Eric Faraday to an off-the-grid location.

When it was all in place, it all relied on Shane following instructions. A good operative, Shane didn't follow instructions well. He embodied the definition of maverick. In some ways, that made him brilliant at what he did for Grant. In others, it made him a good reason to go gray.

Fact was, Grant liked Shane, which is why he gave him the heads-up about Project Sunset. Shane might not care too much about his own survival right now, but he was someone worth saving. Grant couldn't say that about most of his stable. When the thumb drive landed in his lap, he knew who to give it to and why. Brilliance would keep the information safe while oppositional personality traits would make it difficult for anyone, even Grant, to know what Shane might do with it.

Grant Rigby drove down a lonely stretch of I-40 near Duchesne, Utah, when a priority item flashed across his screen. BW scrambled a team to detain Eric Faraday on suspicion of possessing proprietary information belonging to BW. Grant had vaguely expected that to happen over the weekend. It had nothing to do with the thumb drive, he was certain, because that had nothing to do with BW. No, BW didn't want to lose Eric Faraday's skills. They were distracted by their part in the national operation, but that had delayed their plan, not postponed it.

BW had many agency contacts, but when certain names came up, they routed to Rigby. With Grant out of the office, his assistant received the order and moved to protect their asset. He wanted instructions.

Grant pulled over and typed his reply, praying Shane caught his subtext at the coffee shop.

GRANT - He's burned. Bring him into the stable. Be gentle. We might want him in the future.

Grant made much of Eric's depression in the last month. He hoped Baskins would not second-guess the instruction. That Eric disappeared would soon be the least of CSA worries.

"You promised me you'd tell us what was going on as soon as we were definitely out of San Diego," Emily reminded him as he reached for the secure, unregistered cell.

"When we stop tonight, while the kids sleep," he assured her. How to tell her things would never be the same again? He had no idea. All he knew was that he'd laid things out as best he could and hoped his tiny portion of the plan would work. At least his family would be safe for a little while. The rest largely depended on whether Shane Delaney felt restless or not. Grant texted quickly.

GRANT - EF is burned! Both honchos. Hope you're in the wind!

He eased the van into drive and negotiated back onto the highway. Emily stared at the right side view, watching the motor home behind them.

"What is it?" he asked.

"I know better than to ask, but .... Never mind." She sighed heavily.

"When we get where we're going, I'm going to tell you everything." She laughed and brushed a blond lock back from her forehead.

"*Everything*? Twenty years of keeping secrets and you're going to tell me *everything*? Including why my parents and Dylan are on this expedition. How did you convince them?"

"Dylan is amenable to bribery and I told your dad the truth ... more or less."

"And he accepted your version of truth?" Her brown eyes twinkled. She'd accepted his obfuscations as the price of being married to him. Her father and mother had always been suspicious.

"Strangely enough, I think he knew it was coming. We can't talk now. Tonight, I'll tell you what I can and then, when we get where we're going, we adults – and Dylan – will have a real conversation."

She nodded, but a line of worry still creased between her eyes. The secure cell vibrated on the console. He picked it up.

SD - Almost to the mother ship. Thx for the hup x2.

Grant slid the phone back into the box he was keeping it in and sighed. He used his official phone to check-in for Eric's flight to Los Angeles and then onto Thailand, knowing BW would show up to try and intercept their employee. Eric had another reservation at sunset Tuesday, out of Los Angeles, but nobody would be making that flight, so Grant didn't even put an asset on it. He loved it when a plan came together.

Smoke and mirrors meant making the right hand so flashy that the mark never noticed what the left hand really did. Grant couldn't stop the main event, but he could make this little side drama so entertaining that nobody saw through it until it was too late.

Grant looked down at the speedometer and reminded himself to stay just over the speed limit. Smoke and mirrors meant not drawing attention to what you didn't want people to notice. Look anxious, people wonder why. *You're just a family man on a much-needed vacation with his extended family. No need to be in a rush. None at all*

.

Home Pasture

Emmaus

Rob Delaney glanced at the clock. He wanted to mull his reply to Jason Welton's email before sending it, but it was only 2:30 and he didn't have an excuse to leave for the day.

JACE - I recommend a test of the safety valves in the town well house.

Jace was the "county" engineer. Most of the towns in the county used him for their utilities, to review building permits, etc. His construction company was his main priority and Rob sometimes suspected that he suggested certain things to try and generate business for that company. *Who else would do this test?*

Rob's hands twitched over the keyboard. He closed his hands into fists. A small town mayor could get into a fair bit of trouble by rattling off the first thing that came to mind. He pushed back from the computer and turned to the pile of paperwork sitting on the desk blotter.

The Wolf Creek Bridge would probably be completed at the end of the day. Rob felt pride the bridge had been completed under bid and on time without incurring debt. He'd also managed to transfer the landscaping of the town square to the Rotary, resulting in a much prettier park at reduced cost to the town. That had been in his first term. The town rewarded him by electing him for a second term. He hoped the bridge would be the first of several accomplishments during his second term. *Twelve years will be enough, if they are productive years.* He'd frankly been surprised the town gave him a second term after that mess with Shane five years ago. People hadn't forgotten. Nothing like Shane's name to get them whispering. Still, they'd reelected Rob, choosing him over Anders McAuliff, who'd been the one reminding them of Shane's indiscretion.

You need to stop that, his Savior reminded him. *Shane's coming home and if you're thinking it, you're likely to say it sometime when he pushes your buttons.*

Would Shane actually show up? Rob wanted to believe he would, felt ready to talk to his younger son, to lay some anger to the side, but .... *Well, Shane didn't come home four years ago, so why should we get all excited this time?*

Rob's stack of paperwork quickly dwindled. It wasn't even 3:00 yet. He turned back to the computer.

ROB - What is this test for, Jace? I need details to justify it to the council.

The cursor hovered over the SEND icon. *Should I or shouldn't I? Read it again.*

A quick tapping on his office door caused him to look over his shoulder. His elder son Cai stuck his sandy head into the opening of the door.

"You headed out to Wichita?" Rob asked.

"Yeah. I'll be back tomorrow afternoon."

"Good. You should probably be here when ... if ... your brother gets here."

"Well ...." Cai's sea blue eyes twittered.

"What?"

"I think it might be best not to overwhelm him."

"If the situation were different, that might be true, but you have something to tell him and it shouldn't wait for him to find out at the grocery store or over a beer at Callahan's."

"Yeah." Cai's tone dripped with apprehension. "I'm starting to think we made a mistake by not telling him in an email."

"Too late now." Rob grinned.

Cai nodded. At 30, tall and lean, he was clean-shaven and all-American. He'd taken his coloring from Rob -- sandy hair and blue eyes. He graduated from law school two years ago and now split his time between a practice with a friend in Wichita and being the city attorney for Emmaus and the next town over, Mara Wells. Rob was proud of him for planning his life well. He and his wife were living with Rob and Jill while they paid off their student debts. Cai would be free next year. Marnie's emancipation would need longer.

Cai reached for his cell and frowned as he read the text. "Something up?" Rob asked.

"Misty just texted me."

"Misty?"

"Marnie's cousin. She's a waitress at the Barn." Rob nodded that he remembered now. "Shane's a day early, eating lunch at the Barn."

Rob stared at Cai.

"She's sure?"

"He spoke to her."

Rob stood. Cai closed the door and leaned on it.

"Maybe you shouldn't."

"Shouldn't what?"

"Chase him down and catch him unawares. There's a reason he's not answered but one text between us in five years and it's not because he's comfortable with our company."

Rob sighed and admitted Cai had a point. He rubbed the back of his neck.

"You probably shouldn't go to Wichita."

"Yeah, the judge would really like that and so would my client. Besides, it's a cool case -- the farmer selling raw milk to the willing neighbors and the FDA having him arrested for public endangerment. No, I'm going. I think I'm right. Don't overwhelm him. Just think about what I said. You don't want to scare him away."

Cai then shouldered his computer bag and left the office. Rob turned to the window which faced Main Street. He braced his arms on the frames and watched as Wade Lewis' truck made a slow drive down the street. A familiar long-legged stride drew his attention to the bank. Misty was a good informant. Rob watched his younger son enter the brick building. *What to do?*

Cai's warning ringing in his head, Rob didn't obey his first instinct to corner Shane in the bank. He found Shane's Jeep on the side street, parked as if he wasn't hiding. He could see a duffle bag in the back, a water bottle on the passenger seat and a takeout cup for coffee in the console with a logo from a stand Rob sometimes stopped at on his way out of Denver. There were a couple of boxes in the cargo area. Nothing else. *Where's your stuff, kid?* Rob leaned against the passenger door and watched the town go by.

Shane hesitated at seeing him, a mere pause in his stride.

"I don't see any traffic cams." He indicated the roof tops. "Misty?"

"I saw you from my office when you went into the bank." Rob thought he ought to protect such a good informant.

Shane nodded. He leaned against the door next to Rob. He wore sunglasses, so Rob couldn't see his eyes. He seemed taller, leaner, his dark hair clipped short, but still curly. His tan looked permanent. Here in the dog days he wore faded jeans and a green t-shirt with a loose plaid shirt over it. Rob let silence hang between them for a while.

"Are you early or were you planning to keep us waiting until tomorrow?" he finally asked.

"I don't know." Shane's voice seemed deeper, still with that lush quality. "I didn't plan to get here a day early and maybe I wasn't prepared to just show up at the house."

Rob nodded. A million questions ran through his head. *Where have you been? What have you been doing? Where are you going?*

"It's good to see you," he finally said.

"Is it?"

"Yes." Rob scratched the front of his head, where his hair was starting to turn gray along the hair line. "It's hot."

Shane didn't look hot. Rob suspected he'd been spending time in some mighty warm climes the last few years. He was acclimated. Rob had lost that decades ago. The dog days were hot.

"You want to get an iced tea or something?" Rob asked. "We could talk."

Shane let the silence hang for a bit. Rob waited. *Don't let him push your buttons! If he says "beer", let it go and get a root beer. It's not like Callahan's can make you drink alcohol.*

"Sure."

He let Rob lead him to the Soda Fountain. Despite the sunglasses hiding his eyes, Rob could tell the remodeled Woolworth's lunch counter surprised Shane. The store closed before Shane could remember. The block-sized building stood empty for nearly thirty years, but now held the

79

Soda Fountain and a bookstore, while the rest of the block begged for development.

"Wow. I noticed the new houses up on the Heights. Things have grown since I left."

He looked around the Fountain with its red and cream tile and sleek counter with all the images of an old-fashioned soda fountain. He removed his sunglasses as they took stools.

"This was here when the store was open, right?"

"Yes. We used to bring our dates here. Jacob and Vi probably had their first kiss here."

A shadow passed across Shane's green eyes for a moment, reminding Rob that he'd not been here for Vi's death and funeral. They both decided to ignore the obvious, while Rob wondered about the dark shadows under Shane's eyes. Rob ordered lemonade. He ate lunch at home earlier and Shane just ate at the Barn, so after a moment's consultation with the menu, Shane ordered a cranberry smoothie.

"So how many new people are there in town?" Shane hooked his sunglasses in the front of his t-shirt.

"In five years ... about fifty. A 1% gain in a Kansas small town is a miracle."

"Next thing you know, Emmaus is going to have traffic jams."

"We used to." Shane gave him a skeptical look. Since they were keeping it light, Rob opted to keep it light. "When 24 was Main Street and a major highway there were a couple."

"I can't even imagine that. Coming east, once you leave Denver -- it's like no man's land."

"It's quiet." That's what Rob liked about it. "I guess that's why they call it flyover country." The following quiet between them grew painful. "So, you were out west. California?"

"That was my base, I guess." Shane considered something. When Rob didn't rush to fill the silence, he added "San Diego."

"But it was only your base."

The waitress brought their drinks. She was high school aged but gave Shane an appreciative once-over. He didn't seem to notice. At 26, he shouldn't. He sighed.

"You aren't asking."

"Would you tell me if I did?"

"I don't know. I planned to tell people -- even you -- that I was in the military. That's close enough to the truth."

"Is it?"

Shane bought some time by taking a sip of the smoothie. Rob waited.

"You know I didn't go to jail," he said in a low voice.

"Jacob took your Jeep somewhere, so I guessed. You working for Jason Breen made so much more sense then."

"Jason was clean."

"McAuliff was the target all along?" Shane nodded. "How did you get mixed up in all that?"

"My roommate at Embry. His dad. They paid off my student loans."

Rob always assumed that Shane did something illegal to get mixed up with the FBI, so this was welcome news -- but for the dark circles and a curious wariness about his son that he thought he recognized.

"Was it worth it?" he asked.

"No." Shane's answer held no equivocation. "McAuliff wasn't hurting anyone. Jacob was pissed."

"Your grandfather is an anarchist, son. Government overreach always pisses him off. Is that what you've been doing?"

"Yeah, sort of. I'm not really supposed to talk about it."

Rob watched Shane's hands slowly turning the shake glass between them and knew avoidance was not the best answer.

"When you're ready, I'm ready to listen," he assured his son.

"And if I'm never ready?"

Rob sipped his lemonade. It tasted fresh-squeezed, but he figured it wasn't.

"There may come a time when you're the one who will need to listen." Shane's eyes darkened. "You're not ready now."

"It's not Grandpa fighting in the Pacific or you going to the Nam. What I did --. There's nothing honorable, noble or brave about taking money to f -
-."

The bell on the door tinkled. Shane cut off his fierce whisper to look and Rob saw where his hand went when he pivoted on the stool. Jason Breen's blue eyes were cold and piercing. His dark hair thinned back from a craggy face. Rob wanted to step between him and his son, but Shane's hand was behind his back and Rob thought he might not live if he were shot twice.

"Peace, kid." Breen brought both hands up to shoulder level. He held keys in his left. The right was empty. "No need to get blood on the floor."

Shane watched him as he walked to the counter. Breen had apparently ordered a sandwich to go. The transaction took less than a minute. Shane's gaze never wavered, and his hand remained behind his back and under his shirt.

"If you're looking for work." Breen set a card down on the counter near the register. Then he nodded at Rob and walked out. After maybe the count of ten, Shane's hand came away from the small of his back and he turned back to his smoothie. He left the card where it lay.

"You always on, son?" Rob asked, turning back to his lemonade. Shane didn't answer. Rob waited, but not even the pain of silence forced a response. "Okay, fair enough. Your mom has probably heard you're in town by now. You coming home with me or did you book a room at the Super 8?"

"Don't need to." Rob looked at him, curious. "I own Jericho Springs." Rob laughed, but Shane looked dead serious.

"Four years ago?"

"Yeah. Uh, you know of any activity going on there in the last few weeks?"

"I haven't been paying attention." Rob pondered a moment. "It's a ghost town, after all. Why?"

Shane shook his head and shrugged.

"Probably just me being 'on'. Let's play it by ear. I'll go to the house with you and then decide my next move."

"Seems fair." Shane slid off the stool. Rob followed. "I guess I'll meet you at the house in a few minutes then." Shane nodded. They stepped out on to the sidewalk. Shane paused as if to say something, but then turned to walk away. "Shane -- I'm glad you're home," Rob called after him.

Shane broke his stride and glanced over his shoulder, settling his sunglasses in place. "You probably shouldn't be." He continued toward where he'd left the Jeep, leaving Rob to wonder what that meant.

Final Night

Emmaus

Jacob stepped out onto the back porch and let the cooling night breeze wash over him. Shane's dark shadow wavered beside the golden glow that was Glister.

"You two getting caught up?" The yellow Lab's claws clicked softly as he shifted on the stair.

"I'd forgotten about him." Shane's voice sounded hollow, a body sucked empty of its soul.

"He didn't forget about you." It had made Shane smile when Glister threw himself at him like a puppy, tail wagging furiously. His eyes said that hadn't happened for a long time, but Jacob knew there was hope if he could still do it.

"I'm surprised they kept him."

"Why? It wasn't his fault that you ran off. I think Rob especially felt closer to you when he was working with Glister."

Shane swallowed audibly. Jacob sat down on the opposite end of the wide wooden stair and waited. Shane excelled at silence. He always had. Jacob didn't try to outwait him.

"You're not okay, are you?"

"Was your first clue that I'm actually here?"

85

"God's been pricking my heart over you for months now."

"Yeah? Does that mean I'm not damned yet?"

"Not unless you choose to be." Jacob remained a hardcore freewill Baptist.

The infamous Shane silence enveloped the backyard. Jacob let him indulge it for a while.

"I believe in God now," Shane said eventually.

"Man can't spend time where you've been without being confronted by God's existence a time or two."

"I didn't say I thought he was my savior." Jacob listened. "If anything, he's my judge." Shane lapsed into a painfully long silence. Jacob was just about to say something when he spoke again. "You're not correcting me."

"That's your dad's way." Shane's laugh sounded harsh. "God is your judge unless He's your Savior. You decide which He is."

"Say the words, walk the aisle and the world will dawn anew." Shane's voice dripped with sarcasm.

"You know better than that."

"Do I?"

Jacob prayed even during the painful dinner while Jill tried to keep up conversation and Shane hid his meat in the mashed potatoes. Now he offered a quick one -- *God let me speak Your words and let him hear what You want him to hear.*

"It's an inward choice. It's a letting go of your own will and agreeing with Him."

"And my sins -- how's he going to feel about those?"

"He can forgive --."

"No, no, he can't." Shane stood abruptly and fumbled for the stair railing. Jacob grabbed his arm, steadying him.

"You okay?" He felt Shane trembling under his grip. Shane put a hand to his head. The darkness hid his expression, but Jacob smelled cold perspiration from him.

"I didn't get much sleep the last few nights." Shane's voice sounded shaky. "I'm dizzy."

"Jill made up your room. Jericho Springs will be there tomorrow."

Shane swallowed audibly. He rubbed his fingers through his hair.

"Probably best if I don't drive." He didn't move. Jacob waited until the trembling subsided. "It's not as easy as you make it sound."

"It is."

Another long silence ensued.

"If you knew what I've done, you wouldn't say that." Shane stepped up into the porch and away from Jacob.

God, help him! Help me to know how to help him!

Glister nuzzled Jacob's hand as if in agreement. Inside the house, Jill and Rob stood in the kitchen.

"He go to bed?" Jacob asked.

"Pale as a ghost," Jill remarked. "Has he told you ...?"

"Even if he had, I'd keep the confidence. He's here. That's a step in the right direction." Rob's gaze lingered on the dining room door. "You look like a man with some weighty thoughts."

"How do you help someone who doesn't think he needs help?"

"He's not you, Rob. One gift you gave your children that Vi and I failed to teach you is self-awareness. Shane may be good at ignoring that inner voice, but he knows it's there. Just give him a little bit of time."

"He's wound tighter than a drum."

"I'll agree with that. I think he thinks we'd reject him if we knew what he's been doing."

"What has he been doing?" Jill asked.

"If I had to guess ...." Jacob and Rob locked eyes. "War," they said together. "It's a road back from that, but we know how to walk it."

Rob nodded. Jill moved to unload the dishwasher. She's walked a parallel road as a combat nurse. Jacob and Rob moved toward the dining room.

"I'm for bed," Jacob announced. Rob leaned in.

"He's packing. Make sure he knows it's you if you get up to use the bathroom at night."

"I knew that," Jacob assured him, though truth be told, he hadn't seen evidence that Shane was concealed carry. Concealed means nobody can tell. Besides, the kid didn't need a gun even in high school. "Maybe I can get him to go flying with me tomorrow."

Rob smiled.

"You are a wise man, Dad."

"I've had a long time to get that way." Before he climbed the stairs, he asked. "Where's Marnie?"

"She agreed Cai should talk to him first." Jacob nodded and continued upstairs.

The Delaney ancestors built the house with four bedrooms and a bath back when bathrooms were newfangled technology. A later Delaney built the study with the master suite above. Vi and Jacob moved out to the ranch when Rob and Jill started having kids, but when Vi died, Jacob moved back into the long-time guest room in the back corner overlooking the detached garage. The six doors were closed. Light shone from under Shane's door. Jacob smiled to see that.

It's not where he should be, but it's close. Don't push too hard too fast. Patience.

Jacob brushed his teeth. People said he looked younger than 95. He supposed it was because he still had his hair and he didn't wear glasses except to read. He'd always been tall and raw-boned, and he'd kept his weight under control. More frog spots decorated his hands than the last time he looked. Truth be told, he was ready to go home whenever the Lord called him. *Vi is there ... maybe EJ too. I could pass completely happy if I knew Shane would be there too ... many years from now.*

A chill ran down his back like snow sliding off a roof. *What's going on, God? What am I supposed to pray about?* No answer came, but Jacob didn't let that stop him. He prayed as he got ready for bed and even once he was in the covers until he dozed off.

Chicago

Chicago

After an excellent Italian meal, they retired to the suite where a 4-poster be-draped in Egyptian cotton and silk awaited along with a bottle of wine and chocolate-covered strawberries next to a vase of roses.

Drew knew how to treat a lady, maybe because he was one himself.

That is unkind, Nevada thought as she washed up in the bathroom after having sex. *You knew what you were getting into when you started. Just be glad he doesn't invite Lazaro to join you.*

Drew fell asleep, like most men afterward. Nevada didn't smoke every day -- mostly just in celebration -- but she would have liked to light up now. Instead, she picked up a strawberry and savored it. The room was really quite lovely. Drew had excellent taste and he didn't stint on the indulgences. That and his business connections would keep her coming back for a good many dates.

They'd deliver the dragon sculpture to the boutique hotel right after breakfast tomorrow and then begin the long drive back to Emmaus. She wondered that Max didn't ever check credit card receipts or the odometer. Surely, he couldn't be that gullible. *Apparently, he is.*

Drew stirred, opened his eyes and stared around in confusion. "Ah, there you are, my princess. What are you doing over there?"

"Eating strawberries and thinking," she said. It was pleasant in the room even with no clothes on. "I wasn't ready to sleep yet."

"Men are so different from women," he remarked. "I took care of your needs before mine, but still you don't sleep. Very odd. Will you at least cuddle?"

"I'm ready for that, I think." She slid under the covers with him. His anatomy responded as her back pushed up against him. "I so wish we didn't have to get back so early."

"But I must. When you were married, your anniversary was important, yes?"

She wouldn't discuss that long ago mistake with him.

"I know. It's just a thought."

"An errant one for now, dear. I think, though, that we could go another time, if you're up for it."

She was and they did.

Final Breakfast

Emmaus

Alex put his arms around Keri's waist and pulled her athletic back into his stomach. "Don't worry. He's home now," he told her.

"I'm not worried," Keri informed him. He stared at her part as she tilted her head back into his collar bone. "Whatever he's been doing, he obviously knows how to take care of himself. Mom and Dad need to let go of the little boy image. He's an adult."

"Yeah, an adult who left here to avoid a big mess and...."

"His own doing." Keri squirmed around to face him. She was so pretty with her green eyes and honey-colored braid that reached her tailbone. "I love Shane, Alex, but I'm not under the same illusions you and my parents are. He's always been wild. We shouldn't expect him to act like a stable horse. He's a maverick."

"Stu Mackler used to say you can't break a maverick, but mavericks can figure out who holds the nose bag."

Keri looked skeptical but blessed him with a smile.

"We'll see." She sprung up on her toes to kiss him, then glanced at the clock. "Time to go." He released her. She tapped the table and Poppy looked up from her text conversation. "Time go,"

Keri signed. Poppy nodded, finished her text, and began to gather her things.

Brother and sister looked a great deal alike -- tall and blond. Alex was heavily-muscled from farm labor and sports. Poppy was slim as a whip with long arms and fingers, but athletic. She was the normal one in the Lufgren family, born deaf. Alex, with his perfect hearing, had always struggled to feel like he belonged to his parents. His relationship with the Delaneys had been born in that discomfort.

With the women gone, Alex loaded the dishwasher with the breakfast dishes, thinking about his marriage. Unlike most 27-year-old men, Alex had been a parent for nine years, since his parents died in an accident and left him to raise a five-year-old. He'd become real- world-woke-up really fast. In some ways, he'd been blessed by his parents' deafness. He'd been his father's voice over the phone since he could talk. He'd learned a lot just by being an interpreter. Running the farm was not the major struggle for him. Parenting had been the challenge. Raising a deaf child was not incredibly different than caring for a hearing child, in Alex's limited experience, but caring for any child was a challenge, especially when you were 18 years old and had other plans. Thank God for Jill Delaney!

Keri had been the babysitter. Every time Alex needed a moment to himself, which was a lot, she took care of Poppy. She'd been Shane's little sister and Poppy's babysitter. Then she'd gone away to college. Poppy had been mature enough to take care of herself and Alex' interests were becoming more adult as well, so nothing seemed to change ... until Keri came back from college.

Wow! Love at first sight with someone he'd known for twenty years. How could he not have seen her before? It had taken the very outgoing Alex a whole year to work up the courage to ask her out. By that time, Shane had been out of town. That might have had something to do with Alex's bravery. Shane could be protective of his sister in a way that Cai was not. She'd said "yes" and the rest was glorious.

Some things are meant to be!

Ordinary People

Emmaus

Mae Huffman Osimowicz, known familiarly
as Huffy, loved running the register at
Huffman's Market ... except when she
didn't. She enjoyed seeing the comings and goings
of the town, hearing the gossip, smiling at the
babies, and even trying to find that gourmet root
beer someone had tried in Chicago and just had to
have in regular supply. Most people in Emmaus
were just small town folks like she was, peeping
through the hedge at the outside world, glad not to
be living in it. Even some of the newer folks who
built homes up on the Heights were here for the
town and she sensed they'd eventually improve the
herd, so to speak.

This morning, however, she wished she'd slept
in. Not that you could do that when you were a
business owner and your business opened at 9 am
except Sundays. She never slept in, except for a
couple of days after Ellie was born, but her
husband ran the store those days and gave away
half of it, it seemed. *That man ...!*

That wasn't why she was annoyed this
morning, though. Annoyance bore the name of
Katherine Sullivan, the wife of Joseph Sullivan, son

97

of Warren "Ren" Sullivan. Seriously, that woman had used Emmaus as her mailing address for twenty years, yet she never tired of putting down the town. Today, it was about the ecological damage the wind turbines did. Why, Mae remembered when she'd gone on and on about the ecological damage caused by coal power plants and now that the town was working toward making the switch to wind, she was on to something else. Mae just wanted to say "Do you think we should all sit in the dark?" Really, some people just aren't any smarter than sheep.

And now that new-towner, Max Albright, was behind her and agreeing with her. She'd never leave. Neither would Max. What a ridiculously masculine name for a man who favored mauve and manicured nails and shared his life with a roommate of the same sex. *Do they think people in Kansas are that stupid?* They'd been coming to Emmaus Baptist for a few weeks now. Mae wondered how long it would be before they "came out" and demanded special treatment.

The bell at the door jingled and she glanced over to see who was coming in. A face she recognized, young and lean, but she couldn't place. Dark hair and intensely colored eyes that drew attention to themselves. *I know him. Who is he?* She distractedly listened to Katherine chatter on until the familiar face appeared at the end of the line – my, three customers at one time was rush-hour on a weekday morning!

Shane Delaney! Oh, my! That's Anders McAuliff coming in the door! This might get exciting!

"Max, what do you think of the wind turbines?" Mae asked, hoping Katherine would take the hint that she'd over-stayed her welcome.

"Distracting," he said in his light tenor. "I'm all for alternative energies, but some times of the day, the reflection off the blades annoys me. Mostly, though, it's worth it."

"What about the birds?" Katherine demanded.

Max's gray eyes crinkled at the corners as he slid a glance toward Mae.

"Let me just pay for my milk and we can get out of Mae's way." He laid down more than enough for his gallon of milk and encouraged Katherine toward the door. The overdressed Eastern heiress allowed herself to be gently herded. Shane immediately stepped up to the counter, as if he knew Mae was hoping to get the line moving. Mae set aside Max's change to give to him later.

"Shane? Where you been?" she asked as he placed some fruit, bottled water, and pre-made sandwiches on the counter beside two bouquets of flowers.

"Around," he said. He'd always been a guarded kid, not given to chattering.

"Around? Nobody is just around for –uh –must be five years now." Anders scanned Shane's back from head to foot and back again.

"A little over. Mostly been working with the military."

"You were in the Army?" No, she saw that wasn't right. "Navy?"

"Not exactly. I was a pilot for one of the contract firms. How you doing, Mae?"

"I'm doing good. Business is up since new people moved in. Your dad singing his praises?"

"He told me. How's Ellie and ... her boy. Can't remember his name."

"Ellie finally got married and moved to Atlanta. Jos is here with me. He tried to make it work with his stepdad but decided to come home."

Shane nodded. She could see the boy in the man, the same lean cheeks and large green eyes. He had a deep tan and thick hair that laid close to his skull. He was clean-shaven, so his generous lips –the one feature he'd inherited from his father – suggested a woman ought to kiss them. Mae reminded herself that he was young enough to be her son and told him what he owed for his groceries.

He walked out and Anders slowly came forward.

"That was Shane Delaney?" he asked. The mine manager was a few years younger than her, fit and balding. A minority shareholder in the mine, he picked up the four dozen donuts she ordered for every Wednesday morning safety meeting.

"It was. You never met him?"

"I got here after he left. Seems like a polite fellow."

"He comes from good stock. Were you expecting something different?" He handed her his credit card. She ran it.

"I've seen photos." He stared at her a moment. "Now, Mae, don't go spreading it about that I have a problem with him, because I don't. My brother was up to no good and someone had to tell the government. I don't even know for sure that it was him that did it."

"You brought it up in the election."

"Only because a reporter asked me. I never wanted to focus on that. And, there's no hard feelings with Rob either. I just thought the town was ready for more professional leadership. The people disagreed."

She handed the card back to him. He signed the slip, thanked her and wished her a wonderful day and then took his donuts away. Mae wiped the counter down in the lull and thought about the end-caps. *Maybe Alice can help me redo them this morning.* Jos could switch out the overhead signs when he got in from school. First, though, she'd clean the front windows and water the flowers out front.

It is a lovely day.

A Haunting in Beulah

Emmaus

Carl loved the equinox light. There was no better time to photograph anything. The shadows lay perfect and everything glowed golden on film -- even on digital. He eased the Bronco into park and shut down the engine.

Why the graveyard? Ren asked sometimes. Carl hadn't told him. What he saw there didn't show up on film ... except sometimes when it did. And, then he'd wonder. Yes, he was sick. There was that voice in his head that whispered all the time and the scars on his wrists were evidence for when he listened to it, but the things he saw ... were they, could they ... be real? The occasional flicker on the film kept him guessing.

Of course, sometimes he created those vortex shots just for the cool effect. He'd sold some photos that way. It wasn't that he needed the money, but that he enjoyed earning it when he could.

He settled the camera on its strap around his neck, lit a cigarette and looked around him. The sun wasn't too bright just yet. There was a morning skim of clouds diffusing the light. He walked along the road that led through the cemetery. He liked Main Street on a quiet day, junk yards, the prairie, old barns and Kansas ghost towns, but the graveyard was his favorite.

The equinox light just made everything more beautiful. Carl walked around enjoying the quiet and the golden light, taking an occasional photograph until he heard the car door slam.

He knew it was not very nice and probably illegal, but he loved to get pictures of people visiting their dearly departed. He had a whole book of those photos. He never tried to sell them, but sometimes there were the sprites and vortexes that he couldn't explain, the ones that gave him hope that he wasn't completely crazy.

Tall and lean, the young man strode up the hill to the Delaney section of the cemetery. Like a lot of the founding families, the Delaneys had graves in Beulah Cemetery that went back to before the Civil War, the earliest being an infant who'd been stillborn in 1846. Jericho Springs had been the town then. When the town relocated to Emmaus beside the railroad, they'd continued using the hillside.

For a moment, Carl thought the man he saw was EJ, but he knew EJ died a long, long time. No, this had to be Rob's dark one -- the middle one -- who'd been gone for years. Come to visit Vi's grave, Carl supposed. He took a few photos while the young man stood there staring at Vi's monument.

That was a dearly loved woman. It wasn't her fault that she didn't believe me when I warned her. That had been in the early days of the illness and lots of people had scoffed.

Carl froze, watching her uncurl from EJ's grave. He never saw them through the camera lens, not even when they showed up on film. He stared as she came within an arm's length of Rob's boy and then he saw the kid shift his weight and stare at her. She's different and the same. Carl had first seen her as a Vietnamese woman in black pajamas, but now she wore one of those burky things. *The spirit is the same and her name is Death.*

EJ never knew she was there as she rode his shoulder whispering suicide into his ear. Rob's boy recognized her and when he confronted her, she withdrew. She didn't go away. She backed up. It isn't her time yet. *She hasn't gained as deep a foothold in his mind.* But she was there -- that generational demon -- back after all these years.

Carl took some photos, but mostly he thought what Rob's boy would say if he walked up to him and told him what he saw. It's not safe. The boy carried a gun in his back waistband. Carl didn't trust to confront him. She might decide it was time for Carl to die and Carl didn't want to burden that young man with his death. No, he'd figure out how best to handle it.

The young man didn't spend much time before turning to go back to his Jeep. Carl watched her follow him, but far back and then he lost track of her.

The day seemed less bright, though the cloud cover was burning off. Carl lit another cigarette, got back into the Bronco and headed for town.

New Friends

Emmaus

A knock on the screen door caused Alex to look up from the account books.

"Mark, hey." He closed the ledger. "You want some coffee before we get started."

"That would be great." Mark had been working for Alex and several of the neighbors. Today, Alex used him to repair fences. "I wanted to thank you for talking to Mae at the grocery store. Alice says it's a good job and Mae has a small apartment we can rent."

"Great." They took their coffee in travel mugs out to the fence where Alex had already set up for the work. They worked together to bind the fence to a post when Alex asked if Mark spoke to the salt mine yet. "I put in an application."

"And?"

"I haven't heard back from them. It's probably not going to work out."

"Why not? I don't know Anders McAuliff well, but Keri does. We could give you a reference."

"It's gotta get past HR before that."

Alex finished attaching the fence and set his blunt-nosed pliers down, skimmed off his gloves and reached for his coffee. Mark looked uncomfortable, not joining him.

"Is this where you tell me that you weren't born in Texas?" Alex kept his tone light.

"No, I was born in Del Rio to parents who were born in this country." He sighed. "I've got a record."

Alex paused, then took a slow sip of coffee.

"So, you left Texas hoping for easier employment options?" Mark nodded, then looked perplexed.

"You're not unhappy that I didn't tell you?" "You're not running from the law?"

"No. I did my time and my parole. I just got tired of working minimum wage and I took a course in auto repair. I thought that would fix things. It didn't. I couldn't get a job. So, we headed out, hoping maybe we'd find a place where it didn't matter. That was a year ago."

"How do they know?"

"The employers? They ask on the applications. If you lie, they find out when they run a background check and if you tell the truth, they circular file the app."

"That's really unchristian." Alex felt annoyed. "Mind if I ask what you did?"

"I was selling pot -- just small time. Pete was about the age our girl is. I had a job, but I thought of it as an income supplement. It was dumb. I was resupplying when the cops raided my dealer. Lots of money, lots of drugs heavier than pot, major felony. Texas is tough on drugs, so I got 10 years. I did three and then was on parole. I thought it would get better, but landscaping jobs with the illegals were all that were available."

"You don't use yourself?" Mark shook his head. "You weren't stealing stuff?" Mark shook his head. "Keri and I'll talk to Anders tonight. There's a community meeting, he'll be there. Can I be honest with him?"

"Yeah. I'm ashamed of what I did, but I know I can't hide from it."

"I'll ask him to keep it in confidence and give you a shot. You keep the job on your own."

"Thank you! Even if it doesn't work out ... it means a lot that you'd try."

"Don't worry about it. People's past should be in the past. Let's get back to this."

As he pulled on his gloves, a red plane flew low and slow over the farm. Mark shaded his eyes to watch it fly over. The pilot waggled the wings. Alex waved.

"Friend of yours?"

"That's Jacob Delaney's Stinson, which is his 'play' plane. Might be his grandson saying hi."

"Friendly town."

"For the most part. Every community has its bruised apples."

"Yeah, but Houston had drivebys."

"You got me beat there. We had a militia busted a few years back, but they weren't doing anything that affected the town. And then there's Jason Breen. He hires felons, but not for legitimate work."

"I want to be a father to my kids. I feel bad enough that I wasn't around for Pete early on. Hard to do be a father from behind bars and breaking the law is a good way to end up back there."

"That's what I was hoping you'd say. So, we'll work it out. Man who wants to be a father to his kids by not breaking the law sounds like a man who deserves a second chance. We'll work it out."

"Thank you!"

"Yeah, well, thank God more, because He's where I learn compassion from."

"My inlaws are Baptists." Mark's voice strained as he stretched the fencing. "They told Alice not to break her marriage vows when I went to jail. They want us to succeed."

"You a believer?"

"I knelt and prayed with my father-in-law. I'm not a church-goer, but I think the Catholic Church would mark me a heretic. I was baptized in my inlaws' pool by her dad about five years ago."

"I thought there was something I liked about you."

"That's what I thought I liked about you too. Brothers from a different mother."

"There's something to be said for that. So, don't worry about it. We're going find you a job here in Emmaus."

"I believe you'll try." Alex smiled.

The End of What We Knew

Emmaus

Shane looked up from the magazine he pretended to read. Jill had turned on the television.

"I'm going to catch the news since we'll be eating together when it really comes on." She muted the television. "How you doing?" she asked.

The silence of this town is deafening. I'm remembering the taste of gun oil and wondering just how much like Uncle EJ I might be and the more you worry about me, the more I feel like putting myself out of everyone's misery. Sure you really want to know, Mom?

"I had a good time with Grandpa this morning," was what he actually said.

"I didn't expect you wouldn't. He let you fly the Stinson?"

Shane laughed.

"I hold a commercial pilot's license that says I can fly a C130. The Stinson is an elegantly simple machine and my license more than covers it."

"Did he let you fly it?"

"After I begged. And his hands were near the controls the whole time. He let me fly the duster when I was 10 and I was soloing with it when I was 13, but the Stinson ... oh my god!" He saw a shadow expression cross her features. "Sorry. Out of habit in curbing my tongue."

"I didn't say anything."

"You thought loudly. It's your home. I'll pay more attention. After Cai comes home tonight, I'm headed back to the Springs. I won't be a stranger, but I need some alone time."

"Sure." She glanced at the television to make sure it was still commercials or to buy herself a second to hide her disappointment. *What did you think, Mom? I've been living on my own for six years now. Did you think I'd just move home, sleep in my old bedroom for the next year?* He waited for her to suggest it. "May I suggest ... it's something that helped your dad ... he journaled his experiences. That way he didn't have to talk to anyone about it, but he got it out."

I keep forgetting Vietnam. Maybe he would understand if I told him. No! A mercenary is never a soldier. You had a choice he didn't. Maybe writing it ....

Shane nodded to stop her staring at him. Jill un-muted the television as the news started. Shane swallowed illusionary gun oil.

"Good evening. Tonight's news -- sectarian violence in Miristan has exploded into large scale attacks on American facilities. President Merrick Dotson will be speaking from the Lincoln Memorial at 6:30 pm. Microsoft's stock fell precipitously in trading. We'll be back in a moment with the full stories."

Why hasn't Rigby texted me? What did he mean by not doing anything with my assets that I would disapprove of? What is in the generator room and why?

He'd never known Rigby not to answer his text within a few hours. It had been 28. Shane felt so on edge he'd almost texted Mike, before he'd remembered Eric Faraday was supposed to be on a bus to Phuket by now. He felt alone, even in the midst of his family.

Are they still my family? Would they be if they knew the monster I've become?

The normal feeling that had enwrapped him while he was in the Stinson with Jacob had only served to scare him.

I can't let myself be hurt by them.

The anchor droned crap about Miristan, then cut to a reporter who was in a safe location somewhere sort of near. She talked about the hopes and fears of the Miristani. Shane knew none of it was true. He'd never met a Miristani Islamic extremist. He had met Islamic extremists in Miristan and elsewhere, but the Miristani themselves were not Islamists -- yet. Miristan was about BW profits. He recognized one of the burning buildings. The news called it an embassy.

Shane knew it as an American intelligence base. He'd slept in the upper left-hand bedroom during a debrief two years ago. He'd burn it too if he were a Miristani, though he'd have gone after the BW facilities first.

"Makes me glad to live here." Jill hit the mute button when the television cut to a commercial.

"It's quieter." Shane was so used to not talking about what he knew he wasn't tempted to tell her the truth.

"Is that where you were working?" He flinched, which answered her question. He hadn't expected the sort of insight all of them were showing since he got home. It gave him hope that they wouldn't reject him if they heard the full story.

False hope will see your blood on the floor.

"Sometimes." Shane's voice croaked. "I think it might have been a pretty country before people started killing one another there."

"The pictures the news show -- not so pretty."

113

"There's places where there's no violence. That's mostly in the cities. The villages are quiet."

Not all of them. You know not all of them.

A shadow moved at the corner of his vision. Damn! He'd hoped he wouldn't bring her with him, but if she was here now.... Jill turned the television's sound on again Shane turned his non-attention back to the magazine. He hadn't installed a TV at the Jericho Springs Hotel. Maybe that would be a good thing. He didn't need to watch the news.

During one of the commercials, Jill checked her cell.

"Cai's stuck in traffic. He says not to keep dinner. He'll make it for dessert."

Shane was tempted to say he was going to the Springs and he'd catch Cai later, but everybody seemed so certain he needed to talk to Cai. They did have fences to mend.

Fox's news segment was over, and the pundits prepped the audience for the President's speech. *Why did Rigby warn me off big cities by sunset today?* The camera focused on the podium with the Washington skyline blushing toward sunset. Shane's chest tightened. *What's wrong?*

"Good evening, America!" President Dotson said. Jacob called him Breck Boy. The second president not elected by the people. He'd not even been in Congress before President Meyer selected him to replace his vice-president who suffered a heart attack. Dotson replaced Meyer after the assassination 18 months ago. Jacob said he was like Lyndon Johnson on steroids. He started running for office the day he was sworn in and Jacob suspected he'd win the election in November because, like Johnson, people weren't ready for three presidents and four vice-presidents in two years' time.

"As many of you know, Miristan has experienced overwhelming sectarian violence for the last three years. The United States government in conjunction with the United Nations Security Council has demanded that King Farouk Maderis step down and we gave him a deadline of September 25. That was yesterday and King Farouk remains defiant. I sat down with the Joint Chiefs of Staff and Secretary of State Adams and it is the decision of the United States that we must join the United Nations in removing King Farouk from power."

Shane stared at the television, perplexed. Dotson had his fingers in lots of international pots, mostly inherited from previous presidencies, but why start a war with real troops when the covert war with contractors was going so well? Had he missed something during his depression?

"I have instructed Vice President Schultz to call a joint session of Congress tomorrow to discuss the matter and --."

President Dotson looked up from the teleprompter as if shocked to see something as the crowd at the foot of the podium turned in the same direction. Then the camera skewed sideways. Shane saw the backdrop behind Dotson blossom into flame in the second before the camera feed went dead. Jill stared at the blank screen for a moment.

"What was that?" Jill frowned as Shane told his heart to get out of his mouth. *Sunset?* One of the Fox pundits came on, settling his earpiece in place and checking his tie as he sat down in the living room-like setting.

"We've lost the feed from DC. We're not sure what's going on." Another pundit, this one a beautiful brunette, took another seat.

"That was concerning news about Miristan," she said. There seemed to be a lot of commotion behind the cameras. A third pundit sat down. "Joel, how likely is Congress to declare war?"

Joel stammered and tried to explain the partisan issues in Congress, but the beautiful brunette then asked about how US creditors were likely to feel about the costs of armed conflict.

Wouldn't this drive up the national debt further? Joel warmed to the subject now. The national debt now stood at $31 trillion and China was getting increasingly firm that the debt must be paid down, but Dotson showed no signs of actually doing that. Meanwhile the brunette smiled and looked interested while really listening to her earpiece. Her expression moved from mild concern to a much deeper concern. Shane preferred Internet news, so was not really familiar with Fox, but thought she had been a lawyer or something more intelligent than a weather girl.

"We're getting reports that there's been some sort of explosion at the Lincoln Memorial." Joel fumbled with his own earpiece. The first pundit now looked deeply concerned.

"We'll have more information for you as we have it. For the moment, we're going to run an earlier recorded piece by Neil Cavuto. Stay tuned."

Jill spoke in a language Shane didn't recognize. She repeated herself as he forced himself to listen to what she said.

"What do you know?"

Shane wiped a hand over his hair, going to where his bag waited near the door. He made sure he had the right phone and dialed Rigby's number directly. He got voice mail.

"This is ... SD 35781249. Call me! Uh, 5595."
He turned back to Jill.

"Shane, you know something!"

Except for what I don't.

"No, not .... My manager told me something might be going down. But I don't know anything."

"Is that who you just called?" Her cell played a butterfly tone.

"Cai again. He wants to make sure you don't run off."

Shane nodded as he dialed Rigby's other number. This time there was no signal. "Your cell working?" he asked Jill.

"I just got a message from your brother."

"I just called out and now I can't. Does your cell have bars?" Jill looked, then frowned.

"No."

"Try calling someone on the land-line. Dad? Keri?" Jill picked up the land-line.

"It's working." She dialed a number. "Cai's cell isn't picking up." She dialed again. "Jacob's isn't either."

"Try land-lines." *Easy, man. She can't read your mind.*

Shane pulled out his tablet and powered up. The ordinary Internet was there, Twitter feeds lit up. Shane scanned through them, his stomach tightening even more. *Something bad is happening out there and not just in one location.* The word "explosion" kept cropping up.

"Dad's at City Hall, right?" At least twenty messages scrolled across the screen about losing contact with Washington DC.

"Yes, but the meeting must be underway because he's not answering his office phone." She opened her telephone book and dialed another number. Now the Twitter feeds talked about Chicago and Denver. "Shane, what's going on? Your face looks like this is a crisis."

"I think it might be." *Miami, Dallas.*

117

"Tom, hey, this is Jill Delaney. I really need to talk to Rob." She listened for a moment. "He's getting him." Shane nodded, then gaped when the ordinary Internet suddenly cut off to be replaced with an error message. It claimed "Network Error", but Shane's tablet insisted the Internet was still there. Just like that, his mind shifted into a crystal clear state where multi- tasking was more than possible. He could hear Jill on the phone while he remembered complicated passwords and navigated unmapped drives. "Rob, something happened in Washington DC and Shane --. What? Oh, my!"

"What is it?" Shane worked to open the auxiliary web government contractors were given passwords to.

"Rob says they just got a land-line call from Homeland Security activating local area disaster plans." Jill held up a hand while she listened to Rob. "He's hoping you'll stay until Cai gets home. He's going to be a while."

"Right." Shane continued working on his tablet. *Homeland Security ... local disaster plans ... what the heck is going on?*

"What is that?"

"The Internet is down. But not -- it's there, but it's been blocked."

"Is that possible?"

"China does it." Shane breathed a sigh of relief when his CSA email came up. He opened an alert.

All contractors report to your duty stations. National emergency.

Shane sent an email to Rigby.

SHANE - What the hell is going on?

Then he checked his BW account, which was there. *That means something, but what?* A similar email said to report in.

"Shane, answer me! What's going on?"

"I can't tell you, Mom." She frowned. "I'm mostly guessing, and I signed agreements." He tried the ordinary Internet through the specialized web. Shane turned to Reuters when the Associated Press didn't come up.

"The Internet is there. Just not the United States Internet. Oh, my g --."

Multiple cities! Washington DC reportedly gone. Fox News still up in New York. Chicago, Baltimore, Kansas City, Los Angeles, San Diego, Denver ....

"What's wrong? Shane, you're white as a sheet. What's wrong?"

Shane sat down, forcing his breathing to stay steady. Jill took the tablet from his lax hand.

"Oh, my!" she whispered. "God, help us!" she prayed. Now she sat down while Shane gently pulled the tablet from her hand as he stood up.

"I'm going to City Hall. Dad needs to know this. Are you okay?"

"Yes." She ran her hands over her jeans. "How can this be happening?"

I could lie, but why?

"Since Dotson's been in office, things have been pretty scary. They don't put that out on the news, but that's the truth. A while back, my manager told me something was coming, that I should get away from big cities, come here. That's all I know that you don't."

He put his arms around her. It felt awkward, more so when she hugged back. Then she released him and stood up straight. Rob always called that "putting on her combat nurse face." It was easy to forget that they'd met in Saigon.

"Go tell your dad. I'm going to go find Jacob."

"He was spraying a field." His family was safe, but they were all in danger.

"He'd be back by now. The duster isn't rigged for night flight. I'll be fine."

"I don't doubt that, but .... People get a little scary in times like this. You still got that Walther?"

"You're serious?" Shane nodded, meeting her gaze for the first time since he got home. "I'll get it. You?"

Shane, already ahead of her, pulled his 9mm in its back holster out of his duffle and settled it into the small of his back. He settled a jeans jacket over his shirt, grinned at her grimly, shouldered his duffle, and headed for the Jeep.

Separate Paths

Nebraska

*N*ebraska *is even flatter than Kansas,* she decided. No matter how many times Nevada took this drive, she thought the same thing.

Once she got through Lincoln, it just became monotonous, mostly corn fields intersected with hedgerow on either side of I-80. Fortunately, her next sculpture wasn't due until April and it was commissioned in Denver, just a hop-skip-and-jump from Emmaus.

Waco, Nebraska! I wonder if they're as strange as the one in Texas.

The sunset looked glorious off to the south as she listened to a haunting theme song from some popular movie. She pulled into a rest area in York for a much-needed break, parking her van so she'd have no trouble backing out if the big-rig truck was still there when she left. She just straightened from washing her face when her cell phone vibrated. Kim wanted to know if she should make some dinner for her too.

NEVADA - Another two hours, but I'll be hungry when I get there. See you then.

She got some snacks and two sodas from the vending machines, stored some in the van for later and sat down at one of the picnic tables to watch the dying of the day. She'd really rather be eating somewhere else. She could have stopped in one of the towns and at least gotten a burger. Drew drove his sports car separately in order to get back in time for his anniversary. She really did need a man....

"Excuse me," the middle-aged woman asked. "Do you have service?" Nevada blinked at her.

"Your cell? Do you have service?"

"I did a few minutes ago." She pulled out her cell, but No Signal flashed across the screen. "Well, that's weird."

"Yeah. You're the second person I asked, and--"

About a dozen people in her immediate vicinity realized one by one that their cells weren't working.

"Now I'm worried about my kids," the woman complained. "I don't like being out of contact."

"Yeah." Nevada normally didn't worry about Kim, but it did feel like something was wrong. "I should get going. It's probably just a tower or something."

At least Kearney was sort of pretty with the lake off to the right. The low angle of the sun turned its surface into glittering dragon scales. Off the interstate, there were no lights, so as the sun dropped, the road darkened, but she got behind a semi and let him light the way through the corn fields. She didn't ordinarily worry about Kim, but with the cell phone still not working, Phillipsburg looked good. Although the topography wasn't substantially different, she knew there were some slight variations now. Then the truck slowed to a stop and they waited. The seconds ticked into minutes and then the men in Army uniforms came. The one that came to her window asked for ID and wanted to know where she was going.

"Emmaus."

He looked at her driver's license in the beam of his flashlight and spoke into the radio he carried.

"I'm sorry, ma'am, we've been directed to send everyone over to the Walmart to wait."

"Wait for what?"

"I don't know, ma'am. We're just holding the roadblock for now."

"But I don't have far to go and--."

"I'm sorry, ma'am. Please turn off and we'll get you back on the road as soon as possible."

The Walmart parking lot overflowed with cars and people stood around talking, mostly speculating about what was going on. There were national guardsmen on the outskirts, guns slung, but watching them. Nevada shivered even as the evening was still warm.

"Do you know what's going on?" an anxious-looking woman asked.

"They didn't say," Nevada replied.

"I had CB chatter," the trucker said as he joined them. "There was some sort of terrorist attack on Washington DC and Denver."

"I heard the same thing only it was KC," another man said. "Does anyone else have signal on their cells?"

No one did. A clump of ice formed in Nevada's stomach. *What is going on?*

Rumors of War

Emmaus

Rob and police chief Bart Rawlson put road-block barriers in the back of a town maintenance truck when Shane came striding out of the darkness. He'd parked across the parking lot, but something about his stride said he was about something important, even urgent.

Who do you work for, kid?

"Dad, we need to talk." Shane left Bart's greeting hanging in the air.

Rob hesitated. In the past, he'd been dismissive of Shane when Shane had been trying to lead him in a wise direction. His instincts said to ask the boy to help set up the roadblock and they'd talk later, but wisdom suggested he might want to know what the kid knew.

"Bart, keep loading up here. I need to talk to my son."

Bart didn't argue. Rob followed Shane back toward the Jeep.

"What are the road barriers for?"

"Disaster plan calls for controlling the entry points into town, where 24 takes off the 70, east of town at the on-ramp and at the underpass. HLS said it was a terrorist attack in Denver."

"Yeah, well, those sawhorses aren't going to cut it. Not with what's coming?"

"What do you know?"

"That it's not just Denver." Shane didn't look at him. Rob wanted to protest. *He's not kidding!* Rob had no choice but to believe him.

"You checked the Internet?" There were people walking near. He wasn't sure how much he should say.

"Sort of. The regular Internet is blocked with a Homeland Security code, but my employer gives me back-door access."

"So, this is official information?"

He said he was a contractor, but it sounds like he's still working for an alphabet agency. What aren't you telling me?

"Not --. It's complicated." His mouth twisted, suggesting he really didn't want to talk about it. "Since the changes, HLS can only block the United States Internet traffic. They don't control Europe, Asia, etc. Reuters is saying there have been multiple attacks in major US cities and DC is gone."

Rob felt his pulse in his ears like he'd just run a block. The words didn't make sense. "Gone?"

Shane took a tablet computer out of his car and set it on the hood. With a few touches of the screen, he brought up a page.

"This has been updated since I looked last." Shane's voice sounded curiously hollow. Rob looked at the Reuter's homepage. No communication from Washington DC. Fox in New York was reporting Atlanta, Chicago and Los Angeles were also off the air. There were reports that New York police had intervened in an attack on the city.

"Someone bombed the stations. That doesn't make sense. Why would HLS block the Internet?"

"To control the news and slow down the panic. When I left the house, I had the Wichita stations, but by the time I pulled up, they'd all begun playing music. If Cai is in Wichita --."

"My God, no!" Rob felt momentarily dizzy. "He's in Denver, not Wichita."

"Why would he tell Mom he was in Wichita?"

"He didn't say, but he did text me that he was in Denver."

"Where?" Shane asked, eyes on the western horizon.

"He didn't say ... or, er ... he texted that he was stuck in traffic just past Limon. He joked that he had a great sunset in his rearview. That was a half-hour before the HLS message came in."

Shane pulled out a 9mm and checked the clip, then put it back where it belonged. That was a well-practiced move.

"I'll try to find him."

"Shane, that's foolish! You don't know what might be going on in that direction."

"Something I'm imminently qualified to handle, Dad." Shane put the tablet on the passenger seat. "Now's the time to do it before west-bound traffic starts to back up. What's he driving?"

"They'll let east-bound traffic go."

"So, they can stack up at KC? I don't think so. I'll take the Jeep so we can make our own road if we have to. What's he driving?"

"Um, Subaru, I think. Silver with black bumpers down the sides."

"How about license number?"

Rob searched his memory.

"I don't know. Never needed to know. Your mom might have it."

"Never mind. Every minute I delay is a minute I risk being trapped here if the interstate backs up. Dad, those barriers ... inadequate to the situation.

You don't want thousands of people trying to get off the interstate here. Find some jersey barriers or block the roads with tractors but control this thing."

He backed out of the parking place, drove off into the dusk. After a moment of stunned confusion, Rob turned to Bart.

"You know those jersey barriers they were using at the bridge?" he asked. "Yeah. They're supposed to move them tomorrow."

"Get Vern Carlson and ask him to bring three of them to the west off-ramp." "Okay, but why?"

"Honestly? Just in case it's more than just Denver. Then, after you do that, see about getting a couple of the school busses on the other ramp." Bart nodded and moved to comply.

Rob reached for his cell, but he still had no bars. Joe Kelly, one of the deputies, opened a second-story window and called out.

"Hey, Rob. Your phone's not picking up!" "Nobody's is, Joe. What's up?"

"The mayor of Mara Wells is on the phone. I told him it could be a few minutes. He said he'd hold."

"Yeah. Be right there."

Rob turned to Bart, who was on one of the police radios, talking to one of his deputies.

"That's right, three of them. Well, I don't care if Vern's going to grumble. You get over to his place and tell him to do it because the town needs him to."

The streets still looked calm, but Rob had a sinking feeling that wasn't going to last long. He ducked up the back stairs and gestured for Joe to send the phone call to his office.

"Hey, Stan, what's up?"

Stan Osimowicz had been the mayor of Mara Wells for twenty-five years. Emmaus and Mara Wells were sports rivals, but they usually worked together to accomplish big things. The Homeland Security protocols called for them to coordinate in a Level 4 alert.

"Your cell down too?"

"Yes. We're blocking the off-ramp at the 24. What about you?"

"Entrances already secure. Traffic is starting to back up from Denver. You hear anything about what's going on?"

"Well, kind of. If you've got anything sturdier than those sawhorses to block the entrances, it might be a good idea. My kid's a military contractor and he's saying this might be bigger than planned for."

"Good to know. I already blocked the overpass with some tractors, just to be on the safe side for now."

Rob hadn't thought of that. The Emmaus overpass had gates that could be locked.

"Well, good then. We'll talk tomorrow morning for a debrief."

"Sounds good. I'll come to you. Your coffee's better."

They hung up. Rob shivered as the thought came to him that Shane had just driven off toward Denver in search of his brother. Both boys were in harm's way and he'd done nothing to stop Shane from going. If it had been the other way around ...?

Mother's Terror

Emmaus

Jill turned left at Lufgren's Crossing as the evening started darkening the sky. She'd always loved this time of year in Kansas. So, unlike her Native northwest! There was just the slow searing of the grass until at last you knew it was fall. In Seattle, the green just become less vibrant under dreary skies. Here, the sun beat with all its intensity. The dusty, hot earthy fragrance smelled of potency, wild petunia and sunflowers.

A half-hour ago, she'd worried about the used-up quality in Shane's eyes and his meeting with Cai. The world had much bigger problems than their minor family crisis.

"God, there are a whole lot of people who need Your help right now," she whispered as she pulled up beside the duster on the macadam tarmac next to Jacob's hangar. A dozen hangars lined the sides of the Emmaus airstrip, mostly Quonset huts, except for the original one which had started as Barsallai Delaney's barn. Del built the airfield after his crop scorched under the 1930s sun. Jacob owned all of the hangars since their builders let their land leases go over the years. He made a tidy retirement income from their rental. A few had planes in them, but most were storage units. Kansas, once the navel of the aviation world, was flyover country these days.

The hangar's overhead door was still partially open from when Jacob had pulled the Stinson in. The Stinson always parked inside. The duster only got pulled in during its annual maintenance.

"Sun's still up, girlie." Jacob squatted under the Stinson, a rag in hand, wiping down the struts. "He's nervous enough without us making a big shindig out of every meal."

"That's not why I'm here. Something's come up. There's been a terrorist attack on Washington."

The old man rocked back on his heels, staring at her. "Another 9-11. We're going to call this 9-26?"

"Not funny. Rob and Shane both think you should come home."

"And what are they up to?"

"I think Shane went to help Rob set up roadblocks."

"Roadblocks? We're going to keep the world out, are we?"

Jacob crawled out from under the plane, using the wing to pull himself to standing. *You forget how old he is until he's on his knees for a while.*

"Well, I'm done anyway. Already rinsed the duster's tank and fueled her up for tomorrow. Might not fly, though. There's a curious storm cloud over Denver way. Shane volunteer to help Rob or did he get his arm twisted?"

"He volunteered. Jacob, what do you know about what Shane was doing when he was gone?"

"If he won't tell you, it's not my business."

"He says he was some sort of government contractor and he has access to information that we don't have. I saw him access it."

"Then you know about what I know. I figure he can't talk about it and he doesn't want to talk about it, so don't push him to talk about it." He pulled the

132

overhead down and dropped the padlock into place, then escorted her outside of the man-door. He looked up at the sky, frowning to the south. The east darkened rapidly, but the west and south shined glorious with sunset colors.

"What?"

"Dunno. Something. Pilot's instinct maybe."

Jill led the way home in her Tahoe with Jacob following in his 1955 Dodge Ram. The Wichita radio stations were back on the air, saying their national affiliate feed was down. K- Love was just static. *California. Does K-Love even still exist?* Jill tuned to the Fox affiliate, but the news never came up. *God, let Shane be wrong!*

Glister greeted them with a wagging tail. The number 5 blinked on the answering machine.

Jill hit the button.

"Hi, Mom," Keri said. "What's with the cell phones? We're stopping by to say 'hi' to Shane tonight after the City Council meeting."

Beep.

Carl Sullivan left the next three messages. Carl grew up with Rob and they shipped off to Vietnam together. Carl was never the same. You could say the Nam did it to him, but truth was schizophrenia is a genetic disorder. Whatever the cause, he was given to flights of fancy.

"Rob, I'm picking up chatter on the shortwave. I think the Russians are attacking. They got Chicago, San Diego -- and it's just us. Mexico and the rest are still there."

The other two messages reported that DC and St. Louis were gone and then it was Dallas and Houston.

"Well, at least him knowing won't panic people," Jacob said. "I should probably go help Rob."

"No, you should go to Carl's and see what can be heard on that CB of his."

"It's not a CB. It's shortwave. He can hear things from thousands of miles away and talk to them too."

"Right, which is why someone should go find out what he's hearing." Jacob sighed.

"Girl, he's most likely talking to his imaginary friends."

"Shane wasn't pulling up imaginary friends on his tablet, Jacob. Please, go see him."

"I'm going, but if I start smoking again because of it, you can buy my cigarettes."

Jacob hadn't smoked in more than fifty years, but Carl smoked like a chimney. Would it be the equivalent of a contact high?

Surprisingly, Marnie left the fifth message. Dangerous since she knew Shane was here.

"Cai and I were on the phone when the cells cut out. I know I shouldn't be calling, but I'm worried. Have you heard from him?"

Jill dialed the medical center and got one of the nurses and left a message that basically said she didn't know, but she'd try to find out.

She set the phone down in the cradle and then nearly jumped out of her skin when it rang.

Swallowing her heart, she picked it up.

"How are you calling me?" she asked when Shane asked her to describe Cai's car.

"I'm breaking a cardinal rule and calling you with my work cell. Listen, Cai went to Denver to pick something up and I'm headed in that direction to make sure he makes it home safely. Traffic is stopped on I70 west near the exit to Mara Wells. Before I do something drastic, I thought I'd ask for a description of his car. Dad said it was a Subaru."

"Yes. I think he's driving the red one with black bumpers."

"Not the silver one? Why does he have two?"

Dangerous! This is no time for that conversation!

"The silver one is older. The plate for the red one is Lawrence County 473 KTL." Shane repeated it, which she knew would mean he'd remember it as long as Cai owned the car. "The silver one -- just in case -- is Beulah County 279 GLA." Shane repeated that one too. A huge hand squeezed her heart and she felt momentarily light-headed. If Shane is right about Denver, both boys ... oh, no! "Shane, are you sure you want to ...?"

"Don't worry about me, Mom. I've had plenty of experience taking care of myself. I'll call you when I find him."

The phone went dead. After the angry beeping reminded Jill to hang up, she put the receiver in the cradle and then the lights went out.

Family Skeletons

Emmaus

Jacob admitted Carl gave him the heebie-jeebies. He'd been a normal enough kid when EJ and Rob bracketed him, and both had called him friend. EJ had been closer to Ren in age, but Ren had always been driven and EJ preferred hunting and fishing, so he'd ended up throwing in with Carl and Rob. The three of them found all sorts of fun and games all over town and around it.

Vietnam changed all that. EJ shipped out two years earlier than Rob and Carl, but he and Carl come back around the same time. Carl had been crazy, talking delusions about spirits and claiming "gooks" had followed them back. EJ had been silent and tortured, until ....

Jacob still didn't like to think about that, though he knew he saw some of the same symptoms in Shane. Jacob knew they'd need to deal with it later ... after this crisis blew over.

First things first.

"What are you hearing on your radio?" Jacob began when the kitchen door opened. Carl frowned at him.

"I told you on the answer machine -- Atlanta, California, DC, St. Louis – they're off air and there's pilots chattering about EM pulses and "

"Can I listen?"

Carl led him through the kitchen, which reeked of meals long left to rot. The radio room, which had been the dining room when Mrs. Conopher sold the place to Ren, was surprisingly neat and clean. The bathroom was set up for as a photography dark room and the old dining table held the radio and stacks of books and papers, but all organized as if someone besides Carl lived here. His generator kept the radio and a lamp on.

Carl fiddled with the dials on the shortwave for a bit and then let Jacob listen. Surprisingly, he didn't interrupt, and he didn't fire up a cigarette.

"My God," Jacob whispered, breathing a prayer.

"This is a no prayer zone. Though I do understand why you'd want to invoke the grumpy old man in the night shirt this evening. What were those pilots talking about?"

"They're lost without ILS and the airports they should be landing at are not there. Some of them are reporting EMP taking out some of their instruments. Others are reporting that planes have crashed. Have you gotten anyone official on this? Air traffic control or the military?"

"No air traffic control, far as I can tell, but some military chatter. They're mobilizing the National Guard. The Army seems confused. They can't reach their normal command. There's some guy out of Wyoming calling the shots -- Rutherford. None of them know him, so they're a little freaked.

Jacob didn't know a Rutherford either, so he filed it away for later.

"What are they saying about the cause of these explosions?"

"They're talking radiation."

"Terrorism," Jacob groaned.

"You think? Because I think it was our government. What's Cheyenne Mountain doing up and running so quick?"

"That's their job, but you may have a point. I need to go tell Rob about this, although I have no idea what to tell him."

Carl held out a small booklet and a sheath of papers.

"When I first heard about it, I went to a website and printed this off coz I figured nobody'd believe me when the time came. Just got done when the Internet was blocked. It says pretty much what the old manual says. Dig a hole and stay in it for a few days until the radiation clears."

Jacob flipped through the booklet. Back when folks thought nuclear war was survivable, the government put out booklets in how to build shelters. He remembered them being distributed to the schools and Ada brought hers home. The printout was from just a year ago, from DHS giving advice on how to survive a smaller nuclear attack. *The more things change, the more they stay the same.*

"You can take that to Rob. I'm going to start moving my gear into the bomb shelter. I won't let the radio go down for long and I'll keep you informed."

"You seem very calm about all this, Carl."

"I'm on my meds and I've been expecting this for a long time. So, before you go -- I should tell you this because I don't want it on my conscience."

"Tell me what?"

"Your boy -- no, Rob's boy -- the one that looks like EJ."

"Shane. What about him?"

"I saw him up at Beulah this morning. I know people think I'm crazy and I do hear voices, but my illness has never made me see things."

Jacob wanted to say he didn't have time for this, but he remembered what Vi had said about Carl and EJ, so he held his tongue.

"I saw her with him -- the one that used to ride EJ and whisper in his ear that he should hang himself. Shane keeps her back better, but she's following him. And that never means good things, you know?"

You knew it!

Jacob nodded.

"I believe you. Thank you for telling me. I know that took some courage. EJ wasn't your fault, Carl. You know that, right?"

"I know your wife should have listened to me, but she might have if I hadn't been crazy."

"That isn't your fault either, Carl." *And we just don't have time for this now.* "Thank you for all your help here tonight. I'll check back with you from time to time. We need you to man the radio, so we know what's going on out there. Okay?"

"Yup. I'll have to go off air for a while to move the radio downstairs, but not for long. I got the switch all set up."

"You work fast."

"No. I've been planning this for years. It's the illness, you know ... or maybe I'm smarter than everyone else."

"Maybe. Thanks."

"Before you go – I know you don't want to believe me, but ... I got this."

Carl scurried into the bathroom-turned-darkroom and returned with a picture that still smelled of finisher. Jacob stared at it, saw the image behind Shane and then held it closer to the lamp to make sure he really saw it.

"It's not trick photography. I've never had anything that clear before." Carl sounded nervous.

Jacob wiped a hand down his face, feeling the five o'clock shadow.

"I believe you, Carl."

Jacob walked out to the truck, then sat behind the wheel for several minutes, staring at the picture. What Carl described was a demon or the manifestation of depression and suicidal ideation ... different terms for the same danger. This photo though .... Jacob suspected any photographer of Carl's level could doctor an image for a desired effect, but how would he know about this family skeleton? Standing behind Shane on EJ's grave, the Indian woman in the prairie dress held a long warrior's knife in her left hand. Galinda Greyeyes, Vi's ancestress, supposed haunt of many of the men in her family.... many men who died by their own hands.

Shane is in trouble. This is no haunting, just a demon with a connection to the family. And when we're done with this crisis, we'll deal with it. Now we know and you can fight what you know. Not tonight, though. We've got something more urgent to deal with.

Moth to the Flame

West of Emmaus

Just past Mara Wells off-ramp, Shane pulled over to the left-hand side of the west-bound lanes. True darkness hovered minutes away and with the sunset you could make out a column of smoke rising where Denver's light pollution was usually visible. Since traffic wasn't moving, Shane shut off his engine and pocketed the keys before climbing on the roof to spy out the situation ahead.

Multi-lane gridlock. On the other side of the interstate, the east-bound lanes were empty. Shane dropped back down to the shoulder as a trucker came strolling over from behind him.

"You see anything, man?" he asked. Shane noted him noticing Shane's stance and deliberately relaxing. A big man, he could make two of Shane, but in a fight, Shane knew he would take him down in two or three blows. Fortunately, they weren't enemies ... yet.

"No. You picking anything up on your ears?"

"Plenty, none of it good. There's some trucks closer to Denver saying the Army's got roadblocks and there's a whole lot of smoke coming from the city."

"What about east?"

143

"Kansas City shut it down, so even if you could get out of Denver, where would you go?"

"Off the interstate. I wouldn't stay on this rat's maze. HLS protocol has the towns closing the entrances. There's fewer towns to the south. Jump the ditch and take the rural roads out of here."

"Which way?"

Shane opened his mouth, then closed it and looked baffled. The trucker sobered.

"What do you know, man?"

"It's bad. That's all I know."

Shane slipped back into the Jeep and put on his safety belt. He dropped the Jeep into 4- wheel-drive low and cranked it over hard to the left. For a scary moment hanging on the verge, he questioned his own sanity for doing this, but then he was committed. A sharp tug to the right saw him into the bottom of the ditch at enough of an angle not to nose in and then he gunned it up the opposite side to the east bound lane, spraying grass and gravel behind him. The trucker wouldn't have any trouble following him.

Every instinct said he was wrong, wrong, wrong to drive this way, but there was no traffic and he stayed on the inside emergency lane. He put the Jeep back into 2-wheel high and headed toward Denver.

His phone -- the work phone -- rang. Shane picked up, expecting Jill had used *69 to redial him from when he'd called her for Cai's license number.

"You aren't keeping a low profile," Rigby complained, though his tone suggested he wasn't surprised. *You know I don't follow directions well.*

"My brother was just leaving Denver when this -- whatever this is -- happened. He was somewhere

past Limon, the last we knew. Is this a fool's
errand?"

"If he was headed down into Kansas, no. He's
probably fine so long as he doesn't stay there long.
How are you going west?"

"Nobody is driving the east-bound. How the hell
do you know what I'm doing?"

"The miracle of technology. Shane, did you do
what I asked?"

"Yes, like a good little burned-out soldier. I
guess I should thank you for saving my life. You
want to tell me what's going on now?"

"It's the end of the United States as we know it,
Shane. They've hit between ten and twenty cities.
Probably 30 million people died in a matter of
minutes."

Shane couldn't speak for a moment, his pulse
pounding in his ears. He glanced at the
speedometer and lifted his foot slightly. The Jeep
eased off 95.

"You let it happen?" He tried to sound
measured.

"No. I wasn't part of the planning or the
execution. I learned about it – the day I asked you
to meet me at the coffee shop. I couldn't do
anything to stop it, so I chose to get my family and
friends, including you, as far from it as I could. I'm
sorry your brother was in Denver."

"Cai's one person in 30 million. Why weren't
you calling the New York Times?"

Shane eased off the gas again. *Calm down!
Cool! Don't alienate the guy with the technology.*

"You're right, Shane. Morally, I should have. Of
course, my whole family would have been dead, and
the story never would have made press after the
reporter ended up floating in the East River. And
they still would have lit up the cities. This is bigger
than you and me, Shane. It's been years in the

making and our own government was involved, at least in being aware of it and doing nothing to stop it."

Shane hit the count of 10 in his head and swallowed. It took the pressure off his ears. He eased off the gas again, took a deep breath and decided to think instead of feel.

"Nukes?"

"Suitcases. Small, controllable. Meant to disable, not utterly destroy. In ten years, the cities will be rebuildable by people who aren't overly concerned about cancer."

"Who?"

"That's pretty complicated, so not now. We need to hang up soon. A bot just picked us up. I just pumped you -- the real you -- into the system. Did you bring your ID?"

"Yeah. What sort of clearance does it give me?"

"Anything Eric could do. Take a rad badge with you."

"Yup. Will this number work again?"

"Protocol 3."

The line went dead. The code P3 meant use email for the next contact. Shane steered with his left hand while he stowed the work cell in the special shielded compartment in his duffle bag. Ahead, all the lights on the interstate went on like they did every night at sunset and then, thirty seconds later, they all went off along with every light off the highway for as far as Shane could see. Losing Denver had destabilized the power grid and the extra draw from the lights had taken it down. For the first time in Shane's life, he could only see as far along I-70 as his headlights shone.

When he got to the military roadblock at Kanorado where I-70 came up hard against Old 24 at the Colorado state line, he parked, carefully pocketed his keys and strode to the startled young corporal with his shiny rifle and presented Shane Delaney's rarely used intelligence identification. The number of icons on the card crowded the name, but the important one said Homeland Security. Cars stretched out in multiple lanes toward Denver. Now that it was completely dark, Shane could see a glow in the night sky above where the city would be, but somehow it didn't look like the usual light pollution. Besides in a blackout so widespread it took out the interstate lights, would Denver have power? The roadblock had battery lanterns. The Kansas National Guard corporal couldn't have been more than twenty, probably paying for college. Shane couldn't remember a time when he'd been that young ... not seven year ago.

"Can I help you, sir?"

"I'm looking for one of my team. You're letting these people through after you check ID, right?"

"When we get the go-ahead from the commander, yes. You understand, they have to turn south toward Sharon Springs. We've pre-checked about 100 of these cars.

"Red Subaru, Cai Delaney."

The corporal looked in his tablet.

"No, he's not one of those checked in. He could be further back in the queue." "I'm going to go take a look then."

"I need to check with the commander before letting you into the quarantine zone."

Shane continued walking, long legs eating up the pavement. He heard a commotion behind him, but he knew pretending to have authority often meant you could exercise authority. People gave him concerned looks as he passed by them. They had no idea what was going on, but they knew it was unusual. Anyone who moved like they were in charge would get their attention. Twice men rolled down their windows and demanded to know what he knew.

Shane said he was looking for a friend and kept moving. Every twenty cars or so there'd be a squad of guardsmen, rifles over their shoulders, radiation detectors on their chests. So far, everybody was okay, just like the badge Shane wore. Guardsmen checked Shane's ID three times before he saw a red Subaru in the far-right-hand lane about a hundred feet across the Colorado state-line. This was the first group of soldiers who were a mix of Kansas Guard and regular Army. Shane knew he had to move fast when a regular Army soldier started moving to meet the latest Guard corporal he intimidated. Cai startled when Shane tapped on the glass. He got out immediately and wrapped his arms around Shane.

"I cannot believe you're here. Any idea what's going on?"

"It's bad, Cai." Shane kept Cai in the least comfortable hug he'd had since coming back to Kansas. "We need to get away from here as fast as we can."

"Why, what ...?" Shane hushed him. "I don't understand," he whispered.

"It's a terrorist attack on Denver. Dad sent me to come get you." Shane shined his flashlight on the radiation badge. "You're okay, but this is a quarantine zone. We need to leave the car and get back to my Jeep."

"That old clunker is still running?"

"That old clunker is our ticket out of here." He saw movement toward Denver, men and women moving with canisters on their backs. "Get your crap. If we attract attention, my ID may not work."

"You sure we can't drive the emergency lane?"

"Cai, this is a quarantine zone. You're okay, but they're not letting anyone out until they've been thoroughly checked. You can stay, if you trust the military to let you go, but I won't be staying with you." Cai stared at him. The next set of guards was staring right at them while their corporal talked in his radio and shot glances their way. Shane kept his voice low and his body still and let his expression carry the urgency. "Leave the car or you're on your own. I'm not really supposed to be here. I bluffed my way in. We need to go."

Cai began pulling things out of the car and handing them to Shane. "I'm assuming I'm never seeing this car again?"

"Yeah," Shane replied.

Cai rubbed a hand through his straight sandy hair.

"I guess everything else is expendable." He took the items from Shane, stuffing them into his laptop case, which he slung over his back after donning his jacket. Shane took the overnight bag and slung it across his own shoulder. "Where to?"

The soldiers started moving their way.

"Across the median." Cai must have changed after court because he wore jeans and boots. They dropped into the ditch. Shane croached low. Cai imitated him and they were soon out of the range of the soldiers' flashlights. Shane pulled Cai down and held a finger to his lips. They waited. The soldiers found Cai's car. Because it was on the right side of the multi-lane, they looked there.

"Think they think I went to the bathroom?" Cai whispered.

"We should be so lucky." Shane rolled back up to a crouch and led Cai to the upslope. The cars in this area decided to save gasoline by shutting off their engines and headlights. Shane and Cai stayed low until they were in the middle of the lanes.

"Why are they blockading people going east?" Cai asked.

"Stop asking questions until we get to the Jeep, okay?"

"Hey, you guys know what's going on?" a man asked from a nearby car. "Soldiers came through, said it was a factory fire."

"Don't know," Shane told him.

Cai stared at the miles of cars ahead of them. "How are you planning ...?"

"Stop asking questions! I'll tell you what I know when we get there."

Of course, lots of other people had questions.

"Hey, buddy! Where do you think you're going?" a large man asked. He'd been leaning against his car, smoking a cigarette, but now he was in Shane's face.

"Back to my car." Shane spoke in a reasonable tone, pointing eastward. "We walked ahead to ask what the delay was."

"And?"

"It's a factory fire," Cai said. *Oh, great! Now you've done it, idiot!*

"There are no factories," the man snapped, pushing his face toward Cai who stepped back.

Shane did not.

"What's your problem?"

"Nothing so long as you move aside." Shane kept his tone reasonable but firm.

"There's no factory, you idiot!"

"No, there aren't, but that's what the soldier said," Shane agreed. "My brother was just repeating what he was told. You know how it is. Some people want to believe the military aren't liars."

That made the angry man laugh. He went back to leaning on his car. Shane and Cai walked on. Shane had been watching for his Jeep.

"Damn."

"What?"

"They're guarding the car." He checked the rad badge again. *So far so good.* "Look, stay stuck to me like a calf after its mama. Whatever I do, follow. And, please do not be shocked by anything I might do. Okay?"

"Yeah." No sooner had Cai agreed than Shane dropped off the pavement into the ditch again. Cai followed. Shane fished his keys out of his pocket. "When we get there, let yourself into the passenger side and unlock the driver's door. Get the keys in the ignition and be ready to start the car in a second, without drawing attention to yourself. If I sign 'start', start it. If I sign 'go', slide into the driver's seat and get the hell out of here. Be ready for it." He also handed Cai the overnight bag.

"What about you?"

"Don't worry about me. I've got credentials. It's getting you out of here that is the problem."

Two soldiers waited at the Jeep. They straightened when Shane emerged from the ditch.

"Agent Delaney," the corporate said. "Sorry, but we can't let anyone leave the quarantine zone." Shane plucked at his radiation badge.

"We're clean. Nothing to worry about." He could hear Cai doing as told. The private watched him, ill at ease, but not sure what to do about his behavior. Shane fished a business card out from the ID. "Hey, how about you call this number and verify my credentials?"

Rigby, you better have done your job!

Cai now waited in the car. Shane tried to look bored. Somehow doing this as Shane Delaney felt a lot more exposed than when Eric did it. Who knew if there was anyone at the number to answer since the world had ended tonight? Shane waited while the corporal made the call, but as he waited, he slowly worked his way toward the Jeep's driver's door.

He watched the corporal the whole time. When he saw him glance his way and then turn his back as if to prevent him from reading his lips, he signed "start." Cai obeyed. The Jeep, so well-maintained that it was practically brand-new, hummed to life. The corporal started to turn, the private moved to bring his rifle about, and Shane drew the 9mm. He went for chest shots. One. Two. One. Two. They went down like ducks in an arcade. The soldiers at the barriers turned. Shane dropped into the driver's seat, slammed the shifter into reverse and went hard on the gas, pulling the door closed as he accelerated. Bullets began whizzing their way. Lousy shots! No combat experience! Cai screamed, tried to duck, fumbled with his seat belt, grabbed the chicken handle. Shane executed a diplomat's slide, snapped it into 1st and hauled ass. With his headlights off, he could just make out the lines for the center lane. Steering with one hand, he drew his seat belt across his chest and slid the tab into the receiver.

"Good God! How did you...you killed those men!"

"No, but I dented their Kevlar." The Jeep was up to 95 again, but he wanted it that way now. "We can't stay on this road. If they come after us, they'll be loaded for bear."

He slowed down nearing Ruleton, turning into a road leading to a large hotel, then into a narrow farm track between fields that jostled to a county road where he turned north, under the interstate. Cai seemed to be in shock, startling at Shane's wilder maneuvers, but no longer asking questions. Passing Ruleton, Shane continued north, still without headlights. Finally, he turned east until he pulled up beside an old barn, cozied the Jeep between it and an old tractor, just a few yards off the road. He turned off the Jeep, draped it with a tarp he kept in the back, then dragged a couple of pallets over to lean against the Jeep, and put one on top. Then he got back in.

"What are we doing?" Cai had stopped shaking and the panic had left his voice.

"Going dark and silent. Silent. You know how that works?"

Cai's eyes glittered. Maybe Shane annoyed him. Shane opened his tablet, checking for military chatter in the Denver area.

"They're looking. One soldier probably cracked a rib. When ... if ... they come down this road, stay hunkered down, don't move, don't talk, not even whispers. If you need to communicate, sign. They know what this Jeep looks like, but they're expecting us to run, not to just sit here, so they probably will miss us, but not if we make noise."

"I didn't ask you to do that."

"Mom and Dad did. Leaving you there meant leaving you in danger. Staying there meant both of us risking radiation poisoning. I took a risk. Nobody got killed."

"Who are you?"

Shane didn't answer. What could he possibly say that would explain who he had become? He checked the time. It was only eight o'clock, but he felt like he'd left the house two days ago.

"There's a couple of water bottles behind your seat."

Cai felt for them and handed Shane one. A thick silence ensued for several minutes.

"You said I could ask questions when we got to the Jeep."

"Yeah." So far, the search was nowhere near them.

"What's going on?"

"Short story is there was a terrorist attack in Denver and other cities. I know for sure that they hit Washington DC, Chicago, and Los Angeles." Shane checked Reuters. "Atlanta, Miami, Kansas City, St. Louis, San Diego, Portland, Houston, Dallas, Pittsburgh, Cincinnati, Mobile, San Francisco, Phoenix, and Denver. That's what the European press knows so far."

"How are you getting the Internet? It was blocked on my laptop when I tried."

"Same reason they called me Agent Delaney."

"You're some sort of government official?"

"No, not exactly. A contractor, but a national guardsman doesn't know that. Getting in was always going to be the easy part. You're welcome by the way."

"For?"

"They just sent an order out to liquidate the containment zone."

"Liquidate?"

"Kill. I could see up the Colorado way, they were getting prepared for something. They let the cars east of the state-line go, but everything west, which included you -- it's been deemed that you were possibly contaminated and should be processed for liquidation."

He handed the tablet to Cai, who stared at it for a long minute, swallowing tightly.

"I'm ... thank you. But, if they're right   "

Shane used his cell to illuminate the rad badge.

"It's fine." He cracked the window slightly, since it was getting close in the Jeep. Cai followed suit.

"You okay?"

"You know me when the carbon dioxide level goes up." Shane set the tablet on the console between them. A still warm dog day night shimmered outside the Jeep. "It'll cool off eventually. Reuters doesn't have it yet, but my sources say they were nukes. Maybe as many as 30 million people died instantly."

Cai's breathing became harsh.

"How many will die -- radiation -- like that movie --." Nobody got out of Mr. Cottrell's Government class without watching *The Day After*.

"These weren't ICBMs. They were suitcase bombs. Small -- controllable. I read a white paper a while back that claimed a multi-city attack with small bombs would cripple the country, but not radiate things that badly. People lived in Hiroshima after all. They still live there"

"But radiation gets into the atmosphere."

"I'm not an expert, Cai. That's just what I've heard." He picked up the tablet and placed it on the narrow dashboard. "We're going to be here until morning. Might as well hit the rack. I'll take the front."

Cai reached for the door.

"Nope! You don't want to risk the dome light giving us away. Just climb between the seats."

"What if I have to use the restroom?"

"Hold it. Cai, I'm not kidding around. The chatter is starting to pick up that I clearly shot defensively, but there's enough idiots out there, that if they find us tonight, they'll kill us. Shoot first and ask questions never. So, hold it."

Cai stared at him. After a moment, he twisted and dragged his long frame into the back seat. Shane unwound himself from the steering wheel and slid into the passenger seat. He reloaded the 9mm, set another clip on the dashboard and readied the 45 while Cai fumbled around to find a comfortable way to sleep in the back seat. Thus prepared for a last stand, Shane set the duffle bag against the passenger door as a back rest. Silence descended. Shane closed his eyes and saw scenes from *Terminator 2*. He stared out through the window toward the tractor when he heard the Humvee. Cai sat up. Shane didn't move and Cai froze. The Humvee search the roads with directable lights. The tarp brightened, but through the tractor. The light passed on, only to come back a moment later. Shane stopped breathing. He could hear voices over the engine. The Humvee kept rolling. The light passed over the tarp once more from another angle and then it moved on. Shane became aware of Cai's breathing and then remembered how to breathe himself. They sat in dead silence to the count of 1000.

"I think they moved on. "Go to sleep."

Cai's teeth flashed white as if he might say something, but then he didn't. They were quiet for a while. Shane listened to Cai's breathing, waiting for it to slow and deepen. He wondered where Mike and Alicia were.

What's that? A far-off whine played on the edge of his hearing. He felt his entire body become an ear. Cai's breathing paused. It was coming from the west, over the mountains. Shane reminded himself to breathe. *Listen! It's a jet. What's wrong with it? You've been hearing it for a while, but it's getting closer. What's wrong with it? Too low. In the wrong place.*

Then the sound hit them, so hard Cai sat up. The low whine grew into a deafening roar. They both covered their ears. The Jeep rocked with the pounding vibration coming off the jet engines. Light made the tarp glow as wind made it rattle. Shane rolled down the window and stuck his head out, hands over his ears, to stare at the underside of a jumbo jet with its landing gear down and locked, nowhere near a major airport.

It's a 747 going for the interstate. God help the pilot. He's out of fuel and blind.

The pressure on their ears eased as the jet passed. The tarp stopped rattling, the light faded.

"What the heck was that?"

"Denver, Chicago, KC -- they're all gone. Wichita is dark with this outage. He's got nowhere to land, so he's going for the interstate."

Cai swallowed audibly. "Is that possible?"

Shane listened. Miles off now, he heard the explosions. "Theoretically, sure. Practically -- I think he couldn't see."

"Emmaus is in that direction."

"He's beyond Emmaus, Cai. The traffic backed up from KC shortened his runway." Cai exhaled sharply in the darkness.

"The passengers on the plane -- the people on the ground --."

"The good news, if you can call it that, was he was out of fuel. The fire is what kills most people in a jet crash."

"What the hell is wrong with you?" Cai demanded angrily. "Those are people you're discussing so calmly."

This is who I am, big brother. What the hell is wrong with you?

Shane didn't say what he thought. He arranged the duffle bag to support his back better, then listened to Cai's harsh breathing from the darkness of the backseat.

"Yeah. Maybe it should matter more. If you want to pray for them, I won't mock."

"Do you hear how really disconnected you sound?"

"Cai, I *feel* how really disconnected I am. It's not fun and I don't know that there's much I can do about it. The world ended and that feels normal to me. I'm sorry that you're having trouble adjusting.

And, I know that's not normal ... or wasn't before four or five hours ago. You may want to learn how to do it though, because I don't think normal is going to be common for a while." Shane made sure the 9mm was by his thigh and pointed in a safe direction and then eased himself into a more comfortable position. "I'm done talking. Try to get some sleep."

Cai didn't say anymore, but Shane sat listening to his breathing and the distant sounds of disaster for a long time after that.

Community Effort

Emmaus

Jacob showed Rob the nuclear survival brochures when the jet roared past, going for the interstate. Rob made the unauthorized decision not to leave the people trying to get off the interstate at the overpass out there in the open. Jacob, Joe and Bill went from car to car to give instructions to either continue through town and take their chances on the roads or go to the motel and the town would find shelter for them. They told them the truth that this appeared to be a nuclear attack. After momentary panic, most people sobered and made a decision based on their own criteria. People with kids in the car opted to stay, while others had a more varied response. Then Jacob left to tell Jill what was going on and to help her prepare the storm shelter while Joe and Bill left to find the Geiger counters hidden in the cellar of City Hall. Rob was grateful when Bart radioed that Alex had donated an old school bus from his boneyard to block the remaining access point from the interstate. People could walk in, but they'd have to abandon their vehicles. Bart remarked how very strange that there were no vehicles on the interstate. Far to the east, Rob could hear distant

159

explosions. The jet's landing hadn't been successful.

Rob locked the gates at the overpass and drove to City Hall to find Anders McAuliff trying to calm an excited group of townsfolk.

"Mayor Delaney is here, as I said he would be," Anders called out. "Rob, you got anything to report?"

Most of the forty people standing in the City Hall chambers were civil leaders -- the head of the Rotary, Brad Snow the pastor of the Baptist church, the school principal, one of the doctors from the clinic, industrialist Ren Sullivan. There was never going to be a good time to tell them what he knew, but this was as good a time as any to go hip deep in bad news.

"Folks, we don't know all of it. We're getting scattered news from disparate sources and we can't be sure of all of it. What we know is that there appears to have been terrorist attacks on several large cities and they may be nuclear in nature."

He expected them to go ballistic when he paused for breath, but everybody just looked stunned -- except, truth be told, Ren, who likely had communication on his satellite dish from all over the world.

"I had a report that these were smaller nukes and that means they're probably survivable for those of us who are still here. The real risk now is fallout and we have maybe 24 hours to prepare. Every storm shelter, every fallout shelter -- we've got room for about 400 people under City Hall and the clinic. George, how many can the shelter under the school take?"

"Um -- 200, I think, for a day or so. More than that...."

"The information I have suggests we'd only need to go underground for a few days." Alex walked in and leaned against the back wall, his cousin Isaiah beside him. Alex began signing, interpreting. "Storm shelters and basements can be used, but you'll need to pile some sort of mass around and on top of them to block the radiation. It pours off intensely at first and then drops off dramatically. You can get your animals into sheds and pile straw bales, dirt, anything around them, but you got to cover the roof too." Joe signaled that the Geiger counters had been checked and worked. "We'll use the tornado sirens to warn people. We're coordinating with Mara Wells. Alex, you'll have to work something out to warn your folks, right?" Alex held up a thumb to show he understood. "I don't know what else to tell you, folks. You can ask questions, but I don't guarantee I have the answers."

"There are over 5000 people in Emmaus," Louis Chatrain, the head of the Rotary, said. "You've got public shelters for 600."

"People have storm shelters. There are even some old fallout shelters around," Rob reminded.

"Some of us have storm barns," Alex added.

"What about food and other supplies?" Mike LaRoche, the schools' superintendent, asked. "Are there supplies in those shelters?"

"I'm not sure" Rob admitted. "It's only for a couple of days. People can bring their own food."

"The church has a bomb shelter," Brad remarked. "We can hold maybe 50 if we clean the junk out of it."

"That's the important thing to remember," Rob said. "Any building with concrete walls or underground, if you can pile some mass on top will offer shelter."

"You've still got about 800 people who are not protected," Mike remarked. "The last time we did an inventory of storm shelters, that's what we came up with -- about 800 people without cellars or basements and that includes the public shelters. The church was on that list."

Rob felt his stomach lurch. Really? That ... he'd known that the newer houses often weren't built with tornados in mind -- they were on the edge of the Alley -- but 800? .... He swallowed, staring out at the now-agitated crowd, his breath quickening.

"We could get about 500 into the mine," Anders announced. "I'll get a crew building a blockade across the entrance."

"That takes care of the east end of town," Isaiah said, through Alex. "We can squeeze people into our storm barns here and there, but our animals have to come first, and it won't be a fun environment two days in. Maybe 50 can come to us." Isaiah's last sign indicated he spoke for the entire Deaf community.

"I could take a hundred people in the Shack," Ren announced. "The house is brick and cellars are deep." The Shack was what people jokingly called Ren's mansion. *How long have you known?*

"Okay, sounds like we're down to finding shelter for 150 people," Rob said. "That's the people who live in apartments and houses in the downtown area. Lots of concrete there. We'll figure it out."

He spent the next half-hour giving people jobs to keep them busy and keep them out of his hair. When someone pointed out that many of the families had pets, things got tense for a moment, but then Isaiah remarked that people needed to think for themselves and they started to.

With people headed to their respective duties, Rob turned to Anders to thank him for the mine.

"It was actually part of the operational plan back in the 1950s when the mine was tiny and most of the workers lived in the company town." Rob stared at him. "What?"

"There used to be an explosives building there, concrete roof and walls   "

"It's still there. We use it to store bagged salt."

"Might be another place for fifty people to wait it out." Anders nodded.

"I'll get a crew on it. I wonder what other buildings like that there are around town."

"I have a feeling we're going to find out."

"Let's hope we live to make use of what we learn."

Rob nodded soberly and he and Anders just stood there a moment, feeling the enormity of the situation. Then they hurried off to their separate tasks.

Dawn's Early Light

West of Emmaus

Cai woke to bird song and glad to hear it after the roar of the jets the night before. After three of them, he'd expected more. He'd never expected to sleep, but he opened his eyes at the first trill knowing he actually dreamed something about running through the woods being chased. The interior of the Jeep was dark gray and steamy. He smelled sweat.

Probably his own. He lay there several minutes before he could see Shane's shape. He watched the light slowly add details. Shane leaned back against the window, face turned toward the opening, arms loose in his lap. He'd never liked tight places. A stuffy Jeep would have been too much for him in high school. He appeared to be asleep, his taut jaw line darkened with beard, his long lashes brushing tanned skin. Cai saw the 9mm on the console just beside his thigh, inches from his right hand, and thought he'd been smart not to move.

Cai really did have to take a leak but waking an armed man with Shane's obvious skills might hold risks. He was hungry and thirsty too, and his legs cramped from not being able to straighten them out.

165

The dimness receded slowly. Shane took a deep breath. Cai's stomach growled. Shane's eyes opened. Assured that he was awake and recognized him, Cai sat up.

"Is it safe?" he whispered.

Shane shrugged. He drank some water. He checked the tablet.

"Yeah. I think we dropped off their radar. The jet crash diverted them."

Who is this guy? You have Shane's face, Shane's voice, but you are not Shane. You can't be my passionate brother.

Shane put the 45 in the glove box and eased the 9mm into the small of his back before crawling out the driver's door. Cai climbed out the passenger side. They peed at opposite ends of the car, then Shane opened the trunk and rummaged in a box.

"I've got a couple of MREs and some Power Bars," he announced.

"Are we headed home?"

"That's the plan, but we don't know what we're going to find on the way. Best get some food in us before we get going. This one's not too bad if you put the Tabasco on it."

"I'll take your word for it."

Shane gave Cai the breakfast MRE and chose Vegetarian Lasagna for himself.

"These are real military issue." Cai had heard about the carbon dioxide warmers. They just need water. *I wouldn't have believed that.*

"Yeah."

"So, you were working with the military?"

"I signed agreements not to talk about what I was doing." Shane's eyes said there was more to it than that. Cai decided not to push it. The sun peeked between the eastern trees. Cai sat on a cooler while Shane sat on the tailgate. Shane was

166

right about the Tabasco. "So why were you in Denver?" Shane asked after checking the rad badge again.

"I was at an interview. A Denver law firm wanted to hire me for a cush e-commuter gig. It was a second interview. It seemed to go well. I'm thinking I won't get the job though."

Silence hung for a moment as they considered the world. If Shane appreciated Cai's attempt at being real, he didn't show it.

"So, is there something you need to tell me?"

"What do you mean?" *Has he figured it out for himself already?*

"Everybody seemed really certain you and I needed to talk, so   "

"You and I left things in a pretty tangled mess," Cai said, buying time.

"I screwed up, I'm sorry, and I can't take it back."

Where is my brother? Shane doesn't admit wrong-doing, not when it involves me. But he just did. This cannot be Shane.

"You weren't the only one who messed up."

"What are you talking about?" Shane looked honestly perplexed, which confused Cai.

"You came home thinking you had fences to mend, but we both know I owe you amends." Shane shook his head. "Shane, don't! I said some really horrible things that night and for a while before that and maybe you took them to heart, and you feel like you were the only one screwing up. But I screwed up too and Marie should never have put you in the position she put you in."

"You're kidding?"

"No. I'm the one who got her pregnant --."

"Or Dean Armitage was. And, if I'd not gotten drunk at your rehearsal dinner and said those things ...."

167

"You were trying to protect me. It would have been better if you'd said what you said in private, but Marie put you in an untenable position. One thing I've come to realize is that you don't binge drink, so if you got drunk that night, it was accidentally on purpose. You wanted to tell the truth, so you put yourself in a position where you would."

Shane stared at him. A beam of sunlight touched his face, lighting the green of his eyes. He stirred the food in his packet before speaking.

"I shouldn't have done that. I was a stupid jerk and I can never make up for all the shit I pulled."

"Quit trying. I can forgive it. It's the past, you can't change it. Just move forward."

"How?"

"Quit running away and quit breaking their hearts. Stay and let the family heal." Shane stared at the side of the barn for a moment, then laughed in a quick bark. "What's funny?"

"Funny?" He stirred his food again, snorting. "The world ended yesterday, Cai. Where am I gonna go?"

Cai had a hard time taking the next bite of food. He forced himself to swallow. Thirty million people!

"Is there something more?" Shane asked.

You're out of excuses!

"I got one more thing. It's not exactly about you. It's about me." Shane took a bite of his entree, not interrupting. *He's not going to make this easy. Could it ever have been easy?* "When was the last time you talked to Mom to actually talk?"

"She emails me probably once a month, never really includes any information unless I call her back."

"She can call you?"

"I move around too much for that." Shane's eyes were averted. "When I call, she tells me the big news – like Keri and Alex's wedding. I guess you were Alex's best man."

"I stood in for you. How come you couldn't come?" Shane used the food to consider his response.

"My life's complicated."

"I noticed, but so complicated you couldn't come home to attend the wedding of your best friend and sister?"

"Right then, yeah. Six months ago, I wasn't ready for this." He used the sign "we" to show what he meant. "So, what does all that have to do with you?"

Cai swallowed and held up his left hand, knuckles out. Shane glanced at it and then smirked. "You got married."

"In July."

"Good for you." Shane frowned. "But if you're living at the house …. Where was your wife that first night?"

"We thought it best for me to break the news to you, so she did a sleepover with a friend."

"Oh?" Shane seemed to be reviewing something in his head, then he blew his cheeks out in the characteristic Shane going-off-the-dock mannerism. "I don't think I'm so far gone that meeting my brother's wife without him would send me over the edge."

"This one might." Shane gave him a "just let me have it" look and Cai was about to obey when the air filled with another ear-splitting roar as a jet flew low overhead some distance to the east.

"What the heck?" Cai cover his right ear with one hand.

"He's landing," Shane shouted back. "He's out of fuel and he's setting it down on one of the county roads."

Shane began packing up things quickly. Cai moved to help him. This time there was no explosion.

"How do you know that?"

"Angle of descent, direction."

Cai pulled his cell out of his jacket where it lay in the back seat with the thought of texting Marnie.

"I still have no bars, but there's a tower right there." He pointed at the top of a cell tower visible through the trees.

"Power outage and who knows what all else." Shane checked his personal cell. "No bars here either."

"But how do you have wi-fi for the tablet?"

Shane's eyes shifted to the left and then back to look at Cai. Cai's court training told him he'd thought about lying but opted for a version of the truth.

"The soldiers out there have wi-fi too. They've shut down civilian communications in hopes of preventing another attack."

"You know that for sure, or are you guessing?"

"I've seen them do it before." Shane closed the cargo hatch on the Jeep. He checked the tablet again while Cai buckled up. "Okay. There are checkpoints along the Old 24, so we need to take the county roads. There's an old trail here, running up Mission Ridge and then it drops behind Jericho Springs to the railroad crossing and out to Old 24 with only Emmaus checkpoints to deal with."

"How are you seeing all of this? Google Earth?"

"I'm logged in through my agency server. And, yeah, Google Earth is still up, provided you aren't a civilian." He turned the tablet so that Cai could see a standard Google Earth screen.

"What's this?" Cai point at the bright red blob at top edge of the screen.

"That's the jets that didn't make it." He grabbed the loose end of the charger. "Plug it in so it gets charged."

Shane started the Jeep and pulled out from behind the tractor. He executed a right-hand turn and headed east. It wasn't far before Cai could see the thick column of smoke rising from the other side of the trees some distance ahead.

"My God," he said.

"Pray all you want, but when God allows crap like this to happen, it's real hard for me to believe he's on our side."

"I'd argue that with you except you don't believe in God."

"Not true. I am convinced he exists, I'm just not interested in playing footsie with him."

Cai decided to let that go, mainly because he was surprised to hear Shane had become a theist. He'd been an agnostic since junior high and an avowed atheist since high school.

They rode in silence for a while. The fields shimmered with mist as the dew burned off in the warming sun. The road Shane chose started well as it circled north of Mara Wells.

"I haven't been this way in years. I'm surprised at all the corporate fields there are." Shane didn't speak, but his eyes were calculating. "What are you thinking?"

"Inventory of survival needs."

"FEMA will let us know what's needed," Cai said. Shane smirked. *What do you know?*

The Jeep climbed Mission Ridge and at the top they came out on the Overlook, a lovers' leap. Shane stopped the Jeep so they could see the interstate. Emmaus lay near at hand, but beyond, I-90 roiled with smoke from two crashed jets. Another one had landed successfully, its emergency slides deployed.

"I am so glad I chose north rather than south. We never would have gotten past that."

I wouldn't have thought of that. Where has he been that he knows to think this way?

Shane turned the Jeep back on, turned south east along an abandoned railroad siding that would take them to Old 24 and then onto Emmaus.

Spinning

Emmaus

J acob worried about his grandsons. If they'd definitely been together, he felt certain they'd be fine, but there was no reason to believe that Shane found Cai. He'd run off into danger without heed for himself and now.... He'd been gone twelve hours.

Be at peace for I am God.

Easier said than done. Jacob left Jill asleep on the couch after an exhausting night of prepping the storm shelter for nuclear fallout. Rob was doing the same at City Hall. With the inclusion of the mine as a shelter, they could protect the entire town's population, but Rob decided to protect the travelers too and that meant they needed to find shelter for another hundred people. All this swirled in Jacob's mind on the drive to the airfield. *Is there some way to use a portion of the airfield?*

Imagine his surprise when he came to the end of the road that led onto the runway service area and found a commuter jet sitting on his landing strip. The pilot did a crack-up job of squeezing between the buildings on both sides and managed somehow to stop just before the trees.

Jacob drove under the left wing to reach his hangar and park his truck. He calculated he'd still be able to take off and land the duster. A man in a somewhat rumpled pilot's suit, less the tie, emerged from the jet and began striding toward Jacob, who decided to continue with what he'd come for while he waited. He went to the electrical panel at the back of the hangar and hit the transfer switch so the battery back-up would turn on a couple of lights.

He fired up the land-base radio in the office by the time the pilot knocked on the door.

He was a young fellow of about forty, clean shaven, with bright blue eyes.

"Some mighty impressive landing there," Jacob told him.

"Desperation is the mother of aeronautical reflexes, apparently. I was on my last thimble of fuel. You getting anything on that?"

"I'm just warming it up. I use it to file my flight plans when I'm dusting. There's normally a lot of chatter."

They heard only static.

"Gil Maxwell." The pilot held out his right hand.

"Jacob Delaney." *Soft hands*, Jacob thought. *Not ready for what the world is about to become.*

"I don't suppose there's an airport manager or...?"

"I own the field and have only one regular customer. I guess I'm the manager. Where are your passengers?"

"Sleeping, I think. We're almost out of food and water and the toilets will have to be shut down soon. I have no fuel. I can't reach my corporate headquarters. I'm not exactly sure what to do."

"Right. Welcome to the chaos, son. There's fallout coming, most likely. My son's the mayor of the town and he's trying to find bomb shelter space for everyone off the interstate as we speak. Have to include your people in that."

"We were never on the interstate -- thank God, because some jumbos made a huge mess."

"We heard them. You can talk to my son. I'll give you a ride into town."

A shadow darkened the man door. Jacob straightened to see through the office window. The pilot's eyes widened, and he stepped back from the door, holding his hands, palms forward at shoulder level. A disheveled young man glared at Jacob.

"I need a ride outta here," he demanded.

"No need for a gun, kid," The kid swiveled the gun toward Jacob. "I'll give you both a ride into town."

"I ain't going to town. I want to go to Chicago."

Jacob pulled up CB and airline chatter on his home radio last night. His heart contracted painfully. The kid was a homeless idiot. You didn't tell someone with a gun that, though.

"Chicago isn't there any longer, kid." Okay, Gil made two idiots.

"You shut up!" the kid screamed. "You don't know what you're talking about."

"I do. I was supposed to land in Chicago. It's gone."

The kid roared in anger and ran at Gil, smacking him across the jaw with the butt of the pistol. Jacob grabbed a wrench from his tool bag, but the kid pulled the trigger and Gil curled up in pain, then the gun pointed at Jacob, who put the wrench down.

"Look, kid, I can't fly all the way to Chicago. My duster doesn't have that sort of range. But I could get you halfway there." The gun wobbled. "If you don't shoot me."

"What about that plane?"

175

The kid jerked his head toward the Stinson.

"It's an antique and it doesn't work," *Apologies, Jesus, for lying but I am not flying into a nuclear hotspot, not even with a gun to my head.*

The kid looked at Gil, who groaned in pain as a pool of blood formed under him. The kid looked rattled. Like most men, Jacob feared the gun pointed at him, but he'd been in combat and he knew that fear could be controlled. He used the preternatural sharpening of his senses to note details. *Kid's citified ... those tennis shoes were never meant for Emmaus, Kansas. He's off the interstate.*

"That man needs a doctor," Jacob prompted.

"I don't care if he dies." *Younger than Keri, older than Poppy Lufgren. Old enough to do prison time for shooting a man?*

"If he lives, you might not do jail time. If he dies -- that's a whole other story."

"I don't care," the kid screamed. "I just want to go home!"

"I get that. I want my wife. I'm guessing you want your mother."

"Grandmother."

"Yeah? She my age?"

Despite his suspicion, he was also a kid. "Sixties," he allowed.

"Wow, that's young enough to be my daughter. My youngest is 59." *I hope Ada's okay.* "So, you want a plane ride. How'd you get here without a car?"

"I was in a car. It stopped because of the bombs and the army started killing people. I ran."

"Killing people?" *Breathe, old man, breathe. And think!* "Where'd you get the gun?"

"I'm going to shoot you, old man, if you don't stop asking questions and start gassing up the plane."

"Duster's already fueled. That's the one outside. It's got a load of fertilizer in the hopper, so you're going to have to wait for me to pull it or ride on top. It's kind of uncomfortable, but it'll take me an hour to pull that hopper." *There's got to be a little wriggle room for lies told at gun point.*

"I'll ride on top, then."

"Let me call into the City Hall and let them know there's a man here who needs medical care and then we can go."

"And you delay so the cops can come? Hell no!"

"Now, why would I do that with a gun to my head? Kid, you have all the power here. I'm just hoping to save this man's life and then I'll get you as close to Chicago as my fuel will allow."

Jacob waited while the kid considered his options.

"You call, but you don't tell them about me, right?"

"Sure."

Jacob made the call. Joe the deputy answered.

"Joe, this is Jacob Delaney. I have a jet landed on my airfield and a man's been hurt. He's here in the hangar. He's in pretty bad shape. It's a gunshot wound, and no, I don't know how it happened. Can you send an ambulance?"

"Ambulance? I don't know, Jacob. The town is in chaos right now. I'll do my best to get someone out there to take care of it. Do you have a first aid kit?"

"Thanks, Joe," Jacob said. "I'll expect you in about 15 minutes." "What? No, Jacob! Didn't –."

Jacob hung up. Joe would move heaven and earth to keep that commitment, even if it wasn't his idea. Jacob had to get this gun-wielding idiot away from the innocent bystanders in the jet.

Within five minutes, he had the duster powered up and headed down the runway. The kid -- Danny -- was perched atop of the hopper, which wasn't filled with fertilizer, but stank to high heavens from yesterday's residue. Jacob tested the theory the jet would not impede his activity at the field by skimming very close to it, terrifying Danny and, Jacob hoped, waking the passengers who would find Gil.

As he flew over the county road between the airfield and Lufgren's farm, he saw a familiar Jeep and wobbled the wings. Shane stuck his head out the driver's window.

"What are you doing?" Danny demanded, clinging to the hopper with white knuckles. "Little take-off turbulence." *Yeah, that's three lies, Jesus. Getting to be a habit.*

What does an experienced pilot with barn-storming experience do with a gun-toting passenger who is a nervous flyer and not seat belted in?

Jacob took the duster up to a nice altitude, breathing deeply the whole way, and then ... he turned the fabric plane upside down.

By happenstance the gun landed in his lap as he righted the plane. He eased it under his left buttock before Danny figured out what way was up and tried to crawl from the tail to the front, pausing to puke along the way.

"You do not want to hit me, or in any other way threaten me, kiddo, because I'm in complete control over this plane and you will die if I do."

Danny shuddered.

"I'm going to kill you, mo--."

Jacob took another deep breath and turned the duster upside down again. He heard Danny hit the frame on the right side of the fuselage. The plane had a notable tail drag to it after. Jacob executed a corkscrew, feeling Danny slamming around in the back. When he righted the plane, he flipped down the visor mirror to see if his passenger was moving.

You still got it, old man!

"That concludes the entertainment portion of our flight," Jacob quipped. "Please feel free to puke as we return to the terminal."

He watched Danny in the mirror as he turned in a wide loop toward the airfield. When Danny started to move, Jacob executed some less dramatic acrobatics. He saw Shane's Jeep stopped by the hangar. A trail of people streamed off the jet. That wasn't good. He wobbled his wings and saw another pilot waving people off to the side of the runway. He circled, banking sharply to remind Danny he was in charge, and then landed and taxied up to the hangar.

Welcome to the Family

Emmaus

Marnie Callahan held onto the chicken bar as Joe, the deputy, roared the length of the airstrip. The SUV barely cleared the wing of the commuter jet. *How in the world did the pilot manage that?* As they pulled up, she saw Jacob leaning against the duster, an airline pilot trussing a kid up behind the plane and Cai turning from his stride toward the hangar.

She bailed out of the SUV, dragging the medical kit with her. Cai and she hugged briefly.

"Thank God you're here!" she said.

"Shane got me out." *Shane's here? Out of where? Are you really okay?* Cai read her unspoken questions. "Later. You're needed in here."

The lights were on inside of the hangar, which Marnie didn't have time to think about. She'd known at some point that she would encounter Shane. He apparently didn't. *Damn, Cai! Way to wimp out!*

Shane looked like she'd hit him with a 2x4, but only for a moment. Typical Shane, he compartmentalized the situation and set aside the personal conflict for later. He knelt in a pool of the injured man's congealing blood, holding gauze on both sides of the man's side, literally using his arm strength as compression tools. There was no time to discuss their personal situation.

They had a life to save.

"Why am I not surprised that all hell would break loose the second you show up?" Marnie quipped as she kneeled on the other side of the patient.

"I'm not the cause of hell, Dr. Callahan, just a guy trying to survive it," Shane bantered back. "You *are* a doctor, right? At least one of us should have some training."

"You've had some training, I see, but move over and let the doctor take over."

"Oh, I've had reason to use my first aid. Small caliber bullet, maybe a 22 special, lower left quadrant. It's a through-and-through. I don't smell bowel, so I think it missed his guts, but he's bleeding out."

Marnie verified his report, used a compression bandage to take the place of Shane's pressure, installed an IV. She was aware of Cai watching them, ill-at-ease. *Is it the blood or Shane and me interacting? Maybe the blood. Has he ever seen this much human blood before? But, what husband would not be jealousy in this situation? Why didn't you tell him?*

"Did you wash your hands?" she demanded of Shane.

"I rubbed them with antiseptic cream. The gloves too, since who knows how long they've been kicking around Jacob's first aid kit."

She sighed. "I guess that's better than nothing."

The pilot's pulse was thready as he headed into hypovolemic shock. She asked Cai to hold the bag of ringers, but her gut said the patient needed surgery. I should have grabbed some plasma. On the other hand ... Shane is a walking blood bank.

"When was the last time you ate?"

"Within the hour. Why?"

She pulled a blood transfusion kit out of the box. Shane smirked.

"You want to make a withdrawal." He grabbed the rubber hose and began preparing his own arm. "I can give you a unit. This is not a situation where I'm going to agree to weaken myself for a guy I don't even know."

"Totally your own choice."

"And, I'm not saying 'no'." While she hooked up the patient, he hooked up his own arm, barely grimacing as he slid the needle into the artery. *You've done this before.*

Cai and the copilot carried the patient to the SUV with Shane trailing behind at the range of the IV. As a final gesture, he tossed his keys to Cai. Marnie smiled at her husband as Joe drove away from the hanger.

Shane's blood started to show the desired effect on the patient's vitals. She kneeled on the floor and Shane sat with the pilot's legs in his lap.

"Cai said you rescued him. What's happening in Wichita?"

"He was just outside of Denver," Shane told her. *What?* "It was a little hairy getting him out, but we're here now."

Marnie bought time by checking her patient's vitals. "You okay?"

"So far. I've given blood this way before. I'll pull it when I think I need to. While we have a second ...." He took a deep breath, closed his eyes for a heartbeat, then blew his cheeks out. *I remember that. It's a tell for when he's going for it.* "I get why you were angry. You lost your brother and sister because of me. I deserved your rage. Is there any way we can put that in the past and move on as neighbors while I'm here."

Oh, Shane, you have no idea! Cai, I could strangle you! Damn Jill for that stupid idea that she wouldn't tell you this in email. It's not my place to tell you, but ....

"I would be willing to try. Marie wasn't your fault, Shane. When people commit suicide, the loved ones look around for someone to blame. You were handy. It was wrong. If you haven't forgiven yourself for that already, do it now."

Shane averted his eyes.

"So much has happened in my life since then. I don't know how I feel about Marie." His voice grew hoarse. "Josh was my fault, though."

"No. Nobody forced him to get involved in that mess. Even Jason told him not to go that way, but he wouldn't listen." Shane wasn't looking at her. His eyes were on the roadway. He slowly shook his head and spoke in the same strangled voice.

"You have no idea, Marnie. Josh was my fault."

Who is this person?

"Let's just let it rest for a while." They reached the west end of town. "So, why was Cai in Denver?" She tried to keep her tone casual.

Shane started to answer and then frowned. *Here's the naturally oppositional, brilliant man I loved so desperately,* she thought.

"Why is that any of your business?" Shane clearly put fragmented pieces together and then he locked eyes with Joe in the rear-view mirror. Of course, the whole town knew the whole sordid history. It was Peyton Place, Kansas. *How do I say this without turning brother against brother?* Marnie opened her mouth to confess, but Shane's gaze dropped to her gloved left hand. "That's a wedding ring, isn't it?"

"Yes," she admitted. "July, right?"

"Yes."

"Mom and Cai both sent me emails asking me to call. That's how she gives me major news, like Vi dying. That was a year ago. When I finally got around to calling her, Keri was marrying Alex, so I thought it was about that. Was it?"

Perspiration beaded up on Shane's forehead. Marnie swallowed painfully, but the lump in her throat didn't go anywhere.

"We were at graduate school together. We didn't plan it. We were friends and then ... it was more."

Shane took a deep breath, looked at her with storm in the green depths of his eyes   and then started disconnecting the transfusion cannula.

"Maybe we should talk when I'm not giving blood."

"Shane, we didn't mean to hurt you "

"Shut up." Shane's voice was rigid with enforced calm. "You need to give me time to process it. Shut up."

They pulled into the parking lot of the medical center. Marnie had duties. As they transferred the pilot to a gurney, she turned to Joe.

"Stay with him," she ordered and hurried after her patient.

Jazz

Emmaus

Jessica Tully didn't like sitting around doing nothing, but with the power outage, school had been canceled, so she decided to go for a run. It was a little cool when she started at dawn, but within a half-hour she'd stripped off her hoodie and wrapped it around her waist. The town seemed pretty quiet, considering what was going on. Access to interstate had been denied, so where were people going to go? Emmaus was probably safer than the roads, at the moment.

People called her Jazz, a nickname an older brother's lisp created. It was a flashy name for a high-school history teacher, though it played well when she'd been a dancer for a performance group in college. Ballet, jazz, modern, hip-hop, highland – they'd all honed her body to be muscular and strong. Running kept it that way.

Running also kept her from freaking out, which she very much wanted to do. One of her brothers was in Mara Wells, but her parents visited Florida and her other two brothers were gone from home. All cells were blocked. The Internet was inaccessible. She'd pulled one of the three local radio stations up on the battery radio, but they didn't know anything, concentrating on providing information from City Hall to those people who had radios. Jazz paused her run at the Barn to try their pay phone. She'd gotten through to her parents' house in Mara Wells, though her brother hadn't answered. Was it a good sign that land-lines to nearby communities still worked?

Jazz turned at the medical center to head back to her apartment when she saw Joe Kelly leaning over a man lying on the sidewalk. People rarely laid on sidewalks in Emmaus, so naturally she stopped.

"Can I help?".

"I'm fine." The man sounded shaky, was covered in sweat, and pale beneath his tan. Fine might have been an exaggeration. He tried to sit up and spilled sideways. Joe pushed him back down onto his back.

"You should go in and let them check you out."

"I just gave blood. I'm not sick."

"I think you gave too much. Let me get you into the clinic. At least you can lie down for a bit, maybe get some juice or something."

"I can help you get him into the lobby." Folks who knew Jazz did not underestimate her strength. The stranger trembled as they got him to his feet, but braced between Jazz and Joe he walked into the building and collapsed onto a couch in the waiting area. Jazz wondered about the gun in the holster at his back but given that the world had sort of gone crazy last night, maybe she should wonder more why she wasn't armed.

"Does he need medical attention?" the woman at the counter asked.

"No," the stranger said, loudly enough to be heard.

"Yes," Joe said at the same time, adding. "He gave blood to the shooting victim they just brought in. He's a little woozy."

"I'll get some juice. Get his feet up."

The woman, whom Jazz recognized from the grocery store, but couldn't name, disappeared. Jazz grabbed the stranger's left foot, which was the only one on the floor and deposited it on the arm of the couch. He swallowed reflexively, suggesting he might hurl any moment. Joe's radio crackled. Someone wanted to know what to do with the shooter.

"I gotta go. Shane, I'll let your brother know you're here, so just stay down. Jazz, can you stay with him?"

"I don't need a babysitter," the stranger whispered, but Jazz ignored him since he clearly had lost his mind.

"Sure." It just felt weird to tell Joe you couldn't be helpful. Joe honestly became a deputy to help people, which had completely turned her conception of cops on its head. Thanking her profusely, Joe hurried off to the next crisis, leaving Jazz to stare at the stranger who lay on the couch with his forearm across his eyes.

The receptionist returned with juice. Jazz nudged her patient, who lowered his arm to look at her.

"I'm really okay." He looked tan and fit, the sweat on his forehead notwithstanding. He needed a shave and he smelled of sweat and the blood soaking the knees of his jeans, but he didn't look ill so much as tired and pale.

"I believe you. Of course, if you drank some of this juice, I'd believe you more."

"Yeah. I'll try that in a few minutes."

"Shane? Is that your name?"

"Yes. You?"

189

"Jazz."

His eyes twittered.

"Okay, maybe I'm not okay. Did you say Jazz?"

"Short for Jessica. I'm Jazz Tully."

"Shane Delaney."

"Delaney … like the mayor and Marnie? Right, you're the brother-in-law." Shane laughed ruefully.

"I suppose I am." He took a deep breath and let it out slowly. "Okay. I'm going to try sitting up now."

Jazz stayed near should he wobbled again. He had the good sense to keep his feet up on the sofa and to only sit up enough to put his head on the sofa arm. His hand shook when he took the cup of juice.

"You should sip it slowly."

If her treating him like a kid bothered him, he didn't show it. He drank the cup slowly. His hand stopped shaking. He scooted higher on the couch and drank some more juice.

"Do you know what's going on in town since last night?"

"Not really. People are gossiping, but I haven't heard anything official. You?"

"No. The last I heard they were setting up roadblocks to keep the interstate off the county roads." He drained the cup. "I don't really need a babysitter if you have things to do."

"I don't." She indicated her sweat-stained tank top and shorts. "I was running to avoid not having anything to do. How you feeling?"

"Still a little shaky. When Marnie asked me to give blood, I had just eaten, so I figured it would be fine, but I didn't really sleep last night, so   "

"A little busy dealing with the end of the world, huh?"

"It's not the end of the world. It's just the end of life as we knew it."

"I guess that's a good time to stock up on toilet paper." They both grimaced at her deflective humor. "Do you know if it's true?"

"What?"

"Denver? KC?" He sobered. His eyes were a startling green fringed with dark lashes. They didn't look sad. *Calm. He has already wrapped his mind around the truth.*

"And maybe a dozen other cities, yeah, that's what I hear."

Jazz sat down, heedless of his feet, and wrapped her arms around her middle, panic running cold chills through her body.

"My parents are in Florida. They just left last week for Jacksonville."

"I think the terrorist attacks just hit the big cities." He didn't answer immediately. "Miami, but not the rest of Florida."

Jazz took a deep breath and let it out slowly.

"I know it sounds weird. I'm not worried about me or my brothers. But my folks--"

Shane put a long-fingered hand on her bare shoulder.

"I get it. I have friends who were in San Diego. They were supposed to go visit her mother in Santa Fe. I'm really hoping that they did."

He let his hand drop away and slowly unwound from the couch.

"How you feeling?

"Not like I'm going to hit the pavement." He frowned. "I'm stranded."

"What do you mean?"

"Cai has my car ... I think. I don't know how to get hold of him."

"I was running, so   ”

191

His eyes were nothing like his sister's, which were almost an aquamarine. His were dark, but with lighter striation, like a marble, so striking. The dark circles shading his skin under them did not diminish their beauty.

"Using good sense here ... would you walk me over to City Hall? It makes the most sense for me to go there, but I probably shouldn't be doing it without an escort just yet."

"So that tough macho-man thing when you were on the pavement   "

"...was me being really embarrassed that I fainted."

They walked outside to a gorgeous September morning with the promise of more dog days to come. Shane stood quite a bit taller than her, but he walked at a pace, not trying to impress her. It occurred to Jazz that it could be that he was still feeling shaky or it could be good old- fashioned manners.

"I don't know you," Shane remarked as they strolled.

"No. I didn't go to school here. I grew up in Mara Wells. I've been teaching at the high school for two years."

"You and my sister Keri must know each other then."

"We do. I was bridesmaid at her wedding."

"Okay, that's why you look familiar. You're on my parents' mantel."

"Wedding party pictures?" He nodded. "I knew you." He gave her a narrow-eyed stare. "You used to wrestle my brother Geo."

"Geo Tully. Yeah. Okay. Where is Geo these days?"

"In the military at Ft. Lewis."

"They didn't hit Seattle, far as I know."

"Good. He's my favorite brother and I ...." For a moment, she fought back tears and her voice cracked. "Wow, I just never thought I'd feel this way."

They stood there on the sidewalk at the side of the bank while she fought herself back to composure.

"My turn to be embarrassed. I don't usually cry over imagined fears." Shane smiled gently.

"When I heard that Cai might be in Denver ... he and I aren't close, but ... it was this visceral response to go get him. That's what I spent last night doing. Family can motivate us to all sorts of unexpected feelings."

Jazz nodded and they continued toward City Hall. He held the door for her. The Council chambers took up most of the first floor of the building. The assessor's window was closed. Upstairs on the second floor in the police station, the other deputy Tom Henry answered the phones. He waved at Shane and pointed toward the Mayor's office.

The blinds weren't drawn so that Jazz could see Rob Delaney, Cai, the sheriff, the fire chief and the mayor and chief from Mara Wells talking animatedly. Mara Wells didn't have a police department.

Shane sat down on a bench.

"Thanks for walking with me. If you have something to do...."

"Do you mind if I hang out?"

"Not at all." He rubbed a hand over his short dark hair. "What do you teach?"

"History, government and economics."

"Really? Mr. Cottrell finally retired, huh?"

"He had some health issues."

"Do you enjoy teaching?"

193

"I think so. I didn't start out to be a teacher. I really want to get my masters in economic history and teach at the university level."

"That's cool. So, Smith, Hegel, Marx"

"That's right. Keri says you and Cai are hard academic footsteps to follow."

"Naw. Cai is. I just like to read."

"I don't remember … what do you do for a living?"

"Whatever work comes my way. I delivered pizza in high school, detailed cars in college, drove truck, flew cargo planes."

What is it that gets people whispering whenever your name comes up? She couldn't remember and she wasn't about to ask. He seemed like a nice polite guy. The short hair indicated military service to her, but he hadn't said that, so she didn't assume it.

The meeting in the office appeared to be breaking up. The door opened.

"Hey, Jazz!" Mayor Osimowicz greeted. "Your brother Michael asked me to check on you while I was over here."

"I'm fine. Has he heard from our parents or brothers?"

"I'm afraid not."

Shane and Cai talked together. Whatever the topic, looked intense and serious enough to make Mayor Delaney frown. Jazz stepped up beside Shane.

"I should be headed home. It was nice meeting you.

"Hey, thanks for helping." He turned his gaze away from Cai to give her his full attention.

"Well, next time, stay and eat the cookie, okay?"

"I'll do that." Shane looked at the mayor instead of his brother. "Dad, I need to talk to you."

Mayor Delaney deliberately didn't look at Cai before he said "Sure" and Shane followed him into his office. Jazz was already headed down the stairs by that time.

Phillipsburg

Kansas

Nevada unwound herself from the passenger seat at dawn when the National Guard pulled out. As the armored vehicles disappeared down the road, the more energetic of the civilians gathered to watch their taillights.

Nevada went with two of the men to find anyone in charge, but there were no Guard left.

Walmart was still locked up, but someone posted a sign on the door, which they read by the glow of their cellphone lanterns because the parking lot lights were not on.

> Return to your home towns immediately. It is recommended that if you live more than 20 miles from Phillipsburg that you seek emergency shelter instead.

"What is this all about?" Nevada wondered aloud.

"I saw a movie like this, a long time ago," one of the men said. "It didn't turn out well." He scrubbed a hand through his hair, which was already standing on end. "Well, I'm hitting the road."

Nevada returned to the van. She needed coffee and a shower, and she was out of cigarettes. She couldn't bear the thought of drinking soda for caffeine at this hour of the morning, so she decided not to bother. She still had no bars and she was worried about Kim. Emmaus was more like a hundred miles away than twenty, but she wasn't taking the Guard's advice and she didn't think any of her fellow travelers were either.

Her foot rested on the up into the van and her hand gripped the rain gutter when a jet airliner came screaming overhead, way too low.

"Where do you think they're headed?" a woman asked her husband when they could hear again.

"To die," he said. People started their vehicles and got back out on the road in a disorganized rush. The Wichita station wasn't on, but a religious station played music. She almost snapped it off but decided to leave it in case any news came on. She'd driven about thirty miles in bumper to bumper traffic when it did. It didn't make her feel any better about not being able to reach Kim when she learned there might have been as many as a dozen nuclear attacks on cities across the country.

My god, Chicago! Kim must be frantic. Lazaro ... the dragon. KC – what about Drew?

The stream of cars maintained a steady 35 miles per hour, which left her with nothing to do but stay calm and keep driving.

Home Front

Emmaus

Marnie wept. Cai waited for the storm to pass before he asked the pertinent questions. "Why are you crying?"

The mechanical room of the medical clinic was the only private place in the building, a small noisy room filled with the boiler, hot water tank and the back-up emergency generator. The main generator supplied the lights right now, so they could hear one another as she sat on his lap in a beat up chair that the maintenance man slept in when he wasn't fixing things.

"Thirty million people?"

"That's Shane's estimate."

"How does Shane know?"

"He has a tablet that still has the Internet."

"And that sounds rational and sane to you? Nobody else has the Internet, or cell service, or freaking electricity, but your brother has it."

"I've seen it, Marn. I'm not sure where he got all of the figures, but I believe he has access to them."

Marnie wiped tears off her cheeks and snot off her upper lip. What a weird thing to find endearing in a beautiful woman, but Cai found it cute. He remembered the first time she'd cried in his presence and he'd kissed the tears away.

"Shane Delaney, secret agent?" Marnie scoffed. She wiggled a finger into her French braid to scratch her scalp. She'd been on duty for more than 24 hours now and probably needed a shower. "And, this man with the small arms training ... he's angry, Cai. Really angry!"

"I think he's controlled. When he went into the office with Dad, he turned to me and said, 'You could have just told me.' Then he said something really weird. He said, 'Your wife probably would like to see you're really okay.' And he closed the door. I believe you that he was upset when you told him. We gut-punched him. But he had it under control by the time he got to City Hall. Guess who he walked in with?"

Marnie wiped her cheeks dry this time. "Who?"

"Jazz Tully."

"How do they know each other?"

"I think they met this morning. Joe Kelly left Shane in her care when he had to go back to duty. I guess she thought she should see him safely to us in case he got wobbly again."

"Did he sleep last night?" Marnie asked, like she might ask a patient's spouse.

What are you thinking, my lovely wife? Is your concern medical or personal? I really shouldn't be going this way.

"I doubt it. I slept, but now that I think of it, he woke the first time my stomach growled. He was on guard all night."

"For what?"

"Things got a little hairy getting me out of the Denver containment zone. He ... uh, improvised." She looked perplexed. "I told you ... it was like spending the night with a stranger who just looks like my brother."

"That might make the whole sharing a house thing easier for me," Marnie sighed.

"Jacob was the one who invited him to stay at the house."

"Is the old man going soft in the head?"

"No, more like soft in the heart. He's never made a secret that Shane is his favorite. I can understand him wanting to spend some time with him and not really thinking about how Shane or you would feel really awkward sharing a bathroom."

Marnie breathed deeply and let it out slowly.

"I really love your mom and dad, Cai. They are the best in-laws a woman could have ... heck, I wish they were my parents. But you have to admit your family is weird. Your mom is friends with your dad's ex?"

"Mom and Dad were out of here for 10 years after Mae married her husband. They were all adults with other lives when they saw each other again."

"It's weird. Maggie always said it was weird." Cai stared at her, not exactly sure what to say in response. "I know ... my mother declaring anyone else's relationships odd is ... ludicrous." They both laughed. Cai still struggled with her opinion of her parents. He'd been taught to be a great deal more respectful of your elders. "So, is there any chance, given this crisis, that Shane is going to move out to the ranch or ... or something?"

"I don't know. We could move out to the ranch, I guess. Of course, as long as the power is down, gasoline will be a problem."

"Maybe your family can have an adult conversation this evening while I'm working."

"We're going to all get some quality time in the storm shelter for the next few days." Marnie sighed and swallowed.

"Shane in a storm shelter for days with two people he's angry at? No, I think I'm glad I have to be here at the Medical Center."

"You do?"

"Dr. Vashon headed to Wichita to try and find his daughter. Dr. Morton delivered a baby last night, so he's leaving as soon as the shooting victim is clear of anesthesia. I'm low-lady-on- the-totem-pole, so...." She stood up, stretching her back.

"I should be checking on that patient, actually. Thank you for giving me some time with you. Where will you be?"

"Dad asked me to drive around, make sure folks over on the east end are prepping their shelters or know to go to the mine. How are things going here?"

"I put the maintenance crew under Lila Barrett. The school sent some teenagers to help. We'll be ready to go if the sirens sound." She looked thoughtfully at the wall. "You're sure Shane was calm?"

"Sure? No. Seemed to be." Cai pulled her to him as she reached for the doorknob. "Don't obsess over it. He and I will work it out between us."

"I don't know   "

"Really, it will be fine. My wife and her former lover, my brother, sharing a bathroom will be ... very mature and modern."

"All God's children got to love one another," Marnie quipped. That line from *Sexual Perversity in Chicago* was one she often applied to her family of origin. This was the first time he'd heard her use it for his.

"Maybe we're living in a soap opera and don't know it. The Cai Show." She chuckled, then kissed him.

"I think I married you for your hope as much as love." Then she opened the door and was gone. Cai rubbed sweat through his hair and headed to the car. The old Subaru (the only Subaru now) was almost on E, so he turned into the gas station across from the Burger Barn hoping it was open.

A generator put-putted from a shed at the back of the property while a line of a dozen vehicles waited for the pumps. A hand-written sign announced a 10-gallon limit and cash-only. With the Internet down, the credit card machines weren't working. A handful of drivers gathered around the little office, shouting loudly at Vin Barrett and making demands. Cai got out of the car and walked toward them as one man pushed another and angry words filled the air. Cai turned right back around to the car and the radio his father insisted he take with him.

Joe Kelly answered, though he was so close Cai saw him answering the radio as he drove. He pulled in and walked toward the crowd, where someone produced a tire iron and then all hell broke loose.

Panic

Emmaus

Joe Kelly had never pulled his gun in the line of duty, so when Jace Hollander threatened Mick Shumacher with a crowbar at the gas station, his first instinct was to try and talk the two men down. He ended up with a concussion, lying on the ground watching Shell Davis threaten everyone with a rifle until Cai tackled him. At that point, Joe decided to call for backup. Chief Bart and Tom were already in route when a second call came in from the grocery store.

"I think I may need your skills," Rob said to Shane as soon as he turned from the radio.

Knowing that Rob would go alone, Shane agreed.

A dozen people tried to bash their way into Huffman's Market. The window in the front door was already cracked. Rob pulled up aggressively, leaning on the horn, which got everybody's attention. He stepped out of the truck while Shane eased out of the passenger door, keeping the truck between himself and the crowd. He had fifteen rounds, so he could afford to miss once or twice, but probably shooting one person would be enough to quell a small-town crowd.

"What is going on here?" Rob demanded.

A dozen voices assailed him with explanations about why they were committing vandalism. Shane didn't like how exposed Rob was, but he knew he was armed and had no doubt that Rob knew when to draw his weapon.

"That's enough!" Rob roared. A powerful bass-baritone, his voice overwhelmed even their babble. "Mae has a right not to open her store if she chooses. In fact, she doesn't open until 10 and it's 8:30 now."

The babbling started again, and Shane saw Mace Kettridge pick up a double-fist-sized rock to continue his work on the window. Rob stepped back to lay on the horn again and signaled Shane, who brought the 9mm up to rest his elbows on the hood of the truck. When Mace saw the barrel of it leveled at him, he dropped the rock.

"Go home!" Rob ordered. "This is not necessary."

"We need supplies!" someone insisted.

"And you'll get them, when Mae is open. Mace, you'll need to make arrangements with her to pay for the window. Now, everybody, go home! Come back like civilized people in an hour and a half – although if I were Mae, I probably wouldn't open today after this. Now, go!"

"Why the hell should I back down on your say-so?" Mace demanded, which made everyone pause. The fact that Shane pointed a gun at him apparently wasn't enough to scare him. "You think you can come over here and order us around now that we can't call the authorities in to stop you?"

"Mace, when have I ever been the sort of mayor to push people around?" Rob demanded. *Uh, don't play their game, Dad! I'd rather not have to hose down this crowd of townsfolk.*

206

"Right now," Mace insisted. "You got your new deputy here, not even in uniform, waving a gun around, telling people what to do. We've got a right to groceries and gas and you don't get to say who gets what and when."

"Mace, the market belongs to Mae. If she wanted to sell groceries to you, she'd open the door. She didn't. So, go away until she does."

A window opened above Shane's head. His mercenary training had been unable to train gun safety rules from him, so his finger was outside the trigger guard. Mae's voice startled him but he didn't discharge his weapon.

"Go away! My shipment didn't come in last night and people came in and bought stuff. I might not even open today and even if I did, Mace, after you smashed my window, why should I sell to you? Go away! You disturbed my sleep, scared me. None of that is very neighborly. All of you go away now! I'll open when I open!"

Her statement disbursed the crowd. After a few moments, a high school kid unlocked the front door and let Rob and Shane in before locking it again. Mae dressed in sweats and a ratty looking sweater, her thinning brown hair pulled back in a messy ponytail.

"Rob, thank you for coming! I didn't know what to do when they started banging on the glass."

Shane slid the gun into its holster and looked around at the shelves. Some sections looked fully stocked while others were completely bare. Mae explained the train had not arrived yesterday. Shane remembered picking up the container when he'd worked for Jason. Every Tuesday night at 6:00 pm sharp ... except when it ran late.

"It should have been on its way," Shane interjected. "It might be worth it for me to drive the line, see if I can find it."

"I don't know. We might need you in town with what's going on."

"I'm not a deputy, Dad. You probably don't really want me near citizens. I wouldn't have been so nice to Mace had it been just him and me."

"If I weren't the mayor, I'd not have been so nice," Rob assured him. "But you have a point. Maybe you should see if you can find that train. A well-stocked grocery store might go a long way to calming everybody down." He clipped off a key from his ring. "Take the Big I so you can haul what you find home."

Jos, who was Mae's grandson, offered to come with. As they slid into the Jeep, Shane felt obligated to warn the teenager about what it meant to go on an adventure with him.

"You should know that once we're out of town, there's no telling what we'll encounter. I'll deal with whatever that is and you need to be prepared with the knowledge that I've been in a war zone for most of the last four years."

Jos nodded. Shane guessed him at 15. He didn't shave yet.

"I didn't think I was volunteering to go on an amusement ride. People in this town talk about you behind your back," he added when Shane paused. "I want to get the shipment. I'd have gone by myself to find the train if I could drive."

Shane started the Jeep.

"Cool, then. You know who I am and you're not afraid of me. You know how to shoot?"

"I grew up in Kansas. What do you think?"

Shane handed over his backup gun in its holster.

"The tongue clips over your waist band. Keep your t-shirt over it so you're concealed."

Jos checked the gun over, cocked and locked it, then rode without a seat belt to the house, struggling to get the gun comfortable. Jill came out while they prepped the Big I. If she hugged Shane too closely, she also chided him for not calling.

"Things got complicated. Ask Cai when you see him."

They drove the big ranch truck out the mine road to head north and intersect the rail line.

Almost at the township line east of town, they found the train derailed, plowed into a car. Shane suggested Jos check out the freight cars while he walked alone to the front of the train where a very nice German import had been smashed to scrap metal and then burned. The smell rather than any visual evidence told Shane the driver had not survived. There was no sign of the train engineer or his brakeman. After snapping a couple of discreet photos with his personal cell, Shane walked back to where Jos was investigating the train cars. They'd come off the rails, but not that violently, so that most were readily accessible.

"What do you think happened?"

"I think modern society comes with all sorts of electronics that may not hold up well to disruptions in signal. Maybe the car stalled on the tracks, maybe the lights and gate didn't function, maybe the train had a problem. The car driver is dead. Do you recognize what's left of the car?" Jos stared at the photo a moment, but then shook his head. "I think the train crew walked away." Shane stared at the ten cars. "How honest are you?"

"Honest? I don't understand."

"Do you just want your grandmother's shipment, or do you care?" Shane asked. Jos' forehead creased.

"Seems like next week's shipment might be delayed."

The Big-I started life as a commercial truck sometime before Rob went to Vietnam. Jacob bought it to haul goods for the feed store. Mostly it hauled horses and hay these days, rigged with a crane for lifting bales and pallets. Shane picked the locks on the train cars and Jos quickly located the appropriate pallets. Using the crane and a ramp improvised from scrap wood, they dragged three pallets into the truck and were working on the fourth when a tanker truck pulled up followed by a 3-ton panel truck.

Straightening from the work, Shane assessed the situation. He recognized the driver of the tanker truck from his days working with Jason Breen.

"Frank, how's it going?" Frank pushed back his hat to stare at him.

"Shane?!" he asked, as if confused.

"In the flesh." Shane dropped out of the truck and they shook hands. "You here for the diesel?"

"What a mess, huh?" Frank was a long, slender man about ten years older than Shane. "We didn't get this shipment last night and city hall wants us to top off the generators. Can you believe this is happening?"

Nah, this feels sort of normal, but hey ....

"It's pretty twisted." He watched as the three from the panel truck approached.

"Shane Delaney," the youngest of the three men said. "Didn't expect to see you here stealing groceries."

"Not stealing anything, Paul," Shane replied calmly. "We're picking up your aunt's order." Jos straightened from what he was doing.

"Grandmae sent us." Stan Osimowicz' son Paul wrestled against Shane in high school.

"Uh-huh," Paul grunted. "You need to stop, Jos. This isn't yours to take. Dad sent us out here to protect the resources."

"Your dad doesn't have any jurisdiction outside of the township of Mara Wells." Shane calmly evaluating the threats. He knew Rob would want to maintain the cooperative atmosphere between the two towns and he meant to do that if he could, but he didn't trust Paul and he suddenly felt the responsibility of Jos. Frank, an ex-con and former bar fighter, would ordinarily be the one Shane would worry about, but he already wandered down the line to the diesel car. One of Paul's deputies thought he was hiding a crowbar and Paul himself was open-carry.

"That's a formality, Shane. You gotta know the resources have got to be protected."

"I'm not arguing that. We're protecting our resources. You can have the diesel and what we can't get on the truck. But Mae's shipment is going with us."

"No, it's not."

Shane scratched his forehead, pretending to consider Paul's order.

"We're not arguing about this, Paul. We're taking what's ours. Thanks for the visit."

Paul's hand twitched toward his gun as Shane turned away. Shane's foot intersected Paul's solar plexus and his fist sunk deeply into crowbar goon's gut before his foot hit the ground. That quickly, Shane had the crowbar, which he swung at the third guy, who backed off quickly. Paul gagged, rolling on the ground. Shane confiscated his gun. Frank came running back from the tanker.

"You can have this back when we're done," Shane told Paul. "Frank, do not make me shoot you!"

Frank pulled up, hands up.

"Heck, man. I don't even like Paul. Far as I'm concerned, we should only take the Cosco shipment. It was his idea to go for more."

"Good, because I don't want to kill anybody here today, especially not you, but I will do what needs to be done. Got it?"

Jos' eyes rounded like saucers as Shane swung back up on the truck. "Let's get back to work."

They loaded the last three pallets while Paul and Len, the guy who'd been wise enough to back off, broke the locks on the other train cars.

"Can you drive at all?" Shane asked Jos as they were securing the load.

"Not stick."

Shane sighed, then handed the keys to the kid.

"It's in neutral with the brake on. Get in the driver's seat, undo the brake and start the engine and just go with whatever I say."

He retrieved Paul's 357 and the crowbar from the roof of the Big I's cab and headed to where Frank backed the tanker up to the fuel car. He placed the two weapons on the bumper.

"Here's your stuff back," he announced. Frank nodded peaceably, just about done off-loading the fuel. Paul scowled. "Sorry our meeting couldn't be more pleasant."

He turned to go back to the truck. Paul dropped out of the train car and Shane drew his gun. Paul's eyes flared.

"Yeah, I'm concealed," Shane kept the gun pointed at the blue sky above the train car.

"Damn!" Frank hissed. Paul held his hands up, palms out.

"What good would it do me to take you down now?" he reasoned. "The kid would just drive away. My dad will talk to your dad. Next time, this won't fall out this way."

212

Shane laughed what Alicia had always called his "berserker" laugh. Mike always said it scared the hell out of him. Jos slid over to the passenger seat as Shane slid in. They put the train in the rearview mirror.

"Wow!" Jos said. "Paul's not going to take that lying down, you know?" Shane shrugged.

"He's going to have his dad scold my dad. Seriously?"

Jos considered that a moment and then snorted through his nose. "Yeah, okay. Maybe you're more bad-ass than he is."

"Maybe? You don't know me very well yet, kid. You will, though."

"What do you mean?" Shane checked the rearview. Paul apparently decided not to push his luck.

"Well, driving – especially driving manual – is a necessary life skill."

"You'll teach me?"

"Someone has to."

"Will you teach me how to pick locks?"

"No. That's not so much of a necessary life skill."

"So, how come you know how?"

"Misspent youth."

"You would really have taken the Cosco shipment if they hadn't shown up?"

"Of course. Paul's an idiot, but he's right that the resources must be protected. In fact, after we unload this shipment, I'm going back with some guys to see what more we can get."

"Isn't that borrowing trouble?"

"Paul can't carry more than about six pallets in that panel truck, so he's got to make a run to Mara Wells, which means we can get the rest of the goods. If the legitimate owners come looking for them, we can hand them over, but I object to leaving food for looters."

"I'll come with you."

Shane grinned. The kid had the makings of a man who could handle this new world.

A Small Complication

Emmaus

A knock on the door interrupted Marnie as she washed vomit out of her mouth.

"Just a minute," she said, using paper towels to wipe her face. Lila Barrett muscled in and pushed Marnie back before closing the door.

"You need to use this." She set a pharmacy bag on the counter.

"What is it?"

"You know." Her brown eyes weighed as Marnie shook her head. She pursed her full lips. "Girl, this is the third day in a row you've gone to the bathroom to throw up. Given your age, I'm ruling out stomach cancer and you've been inoculated against the usual diseases, so that narrows the field. Take the test and you'll know for certain."

"You're kidding, right? We use contraception."

"Yeah, well, that usually works, but sometimes it doesn't. So, take the test."

"Fine, but I'm not pregnant. There's no way."

"If you're having sex, there's a way. I'll leave you to it." Lila closed the door and Marnie locked it.

"No way!" She sighed and pulled the box out of the bag. She'd been sexually active since the summer before high school. She'd always used the

215

same method of contraception and there'd never been any scares. She and Cai decided they didn't want children until after they'd paid off their school debts. But she had thrown up three days in a row and, truth be told, she had other symptoms.

What to do about this if the test were positive? *Thirty million people died last night.*

This was not the best time to bring a kid into the world.

Is there ever a good time?

What would Cai say? What would Shane say? It isn't really any of his concern, but it might complicate things more than necessary. *And Maggie will freak!*

Of course, there were two bars. She'd known all along that there would be. The wedding had been 11 weeks ago tomorrow and she hadn't had a period since then. There was no reason to believe she'd been pregnant before the wedding. That would be consistent with Cai's history with Callahan girls – the first time would be enough.

She wiped a scatter of tears from her cheeks, undecided to be happy or sad, gathered up the evidence and went to find Lila. This was a complication she had not expected, and she wasn't altogether sure if she shouldn't just make a wise choice and be done with it.

Widows & Orphans

Emmaus

Cai canvassed the east end of town to spread the news about the shelters but the mine's security staff had already done much of that. His arc finally brought him to the north side of the Delaney property where the ranch sat.

It had been a ranch once when the Delaneys ran a few head of cattle, before Jacob's brother died in World War Two. Jacob kept it for the horses and he and Vi lived in the house until her death. She'd enjoyed the creek. Now the house was rented out, but the Delaney horses still occupied the concrete barn.

The tenant's daughter showed up as Cai tried to start the tractor with the idea of piling straw bales against the doors.

"Um, do you know what's going on?" he asked her.

"The news said it was a terrorist attack. There's a storm shelter here. I stacked mattresses on top and ... hey, you're the landlord's son, right?"

"Cai Delaney. Where are your parents?"

"My mother didn't come home last night," she said in a tight voice. Her slender face bore the mark of tears.

"Where was she?"

"Chicago."

His court training had taught him how to control his expressions without thinking about it, but his heart turned over with a dull thud.

"She was on I35 headed back when she texted me just before sundown." Cai breathed.

"She probably got caught up in one of the roadblocks. Do you have food for the shelter?"

"I took some canned goods down and peanut butter and bread."

Cai turned to stare at the backlit shadow in the door. His gait identified Jacob.

"Great minds and all that," the old man said. "I've got so much stored upstairs, I doubt we'll need to add any mass, but I'm going to check. Where's your mother, young lady?"

"I don't know. I've got the shelter ready, though."

"You shouldn't stay here alone."

"She's a little short on food too," Cai explained.

"I want to be here when my mom gets here."

"Cai, make sure she has water and other survival items in the shelter. I think I've got some storage food upstairs."

Cai knew Jacob. The old man could read people so well. He didn't want to panic Kim. This was probably going to end with Cai dragging the girl off to the City Hall shelter.

Kim had actually followed the instructions on Emmaus radio pretty well and had food, water, blankets, a lantern and other items in the little shelter under the house. Jacob returned with a box of freeze-dried foods and a report that he thought the horses would be sufficiently protected in their bunker-like barn. The three of them worked together to make sure the horses had water and food for the next few days and then got to work blocking the wooden walls. Cai mentally rehearsed how to pry Kim loose of her home when a white van came tearing up the driveway and a woman with bright-blond threw herself out of it.

"I'm going to the Heights to make sure everybody got the message," Cai told Jacob, who nodded. "Shane knows, by the way."

"Yup! I did say to email him, didn't I?"

"Yeah, but I didn't, and it's done now. And he acted surprisingly like a grown-up."

"Good. Your brother's got enough to keep him busy right now. You guys will get through this ... if the radiation don't kill us. I'll head back to get another assignment from your father soon as I'm done here. Get going."

Cai got back in the Subaru to head to the next phase of his mission, leaving Jacob to deal with the Randolph women.

Disconnected

Emmaus

Jacob couldn't believe the National Broadcast radio had been transferred to the Internet, which was not accessible at the moment. Rob told him that at City Hall before Maggie Callahan called to report she'd gotten something on the satellite television at the restaurant.

"Whose stupid idea was that?" he asked Rob as Rob drove toward Callahan's.

"Homeland Security. The mayors that objected were mocked as old-fashioned and hopelessly out of touch." Jacob shook his head. "It gets worse. My assigned contact number is a Denver area code."

"And the backup?"

"Chicago." *We're on our own!* "So, I tried Wichita and I'm getting a constant busy signal." *I admire your persistence, but we're on our own.* "I've left four messages for the National Guard. The phone tree didn't work this morning. I got an actual human. But the last two messages have gone right to voice mail."

It's like one of those old Twilight Zone episodes.

"What's your plan?"

Rob made an "I'm-not-there-yet face" and parked. Jacob had a sense of what his own plan

221

would be, but he hadn't been the mayor in thirty-five years and Rob didn't need his daddy telling him what to do ... yet.

Maggie Callahan ran the only bar in Emmaus, a pleasant wood-paneled building with a central bar surrounded by tables and then booths and a large screen television usually used for football games. She hosted a band on Friday and Saturday nights and had a full meal menu.

Jacob could hear the generator putt-putting in the back lot as they entered the building. A dozen people gathered there, including Jason Breen, Maggie's semi-estranged common-law mate – Marnie's father. The television picked up a broadcast from a Spanish language station.

A video clip displayed behind the announcer, people running and screaming as a bright light and cloud appeared on the horizon. Shaky cell phone video followed as the announcer added commentary in Spanish.

"That's Chicago." Jason saw Rob and nodded peaceably.

"Anyone here speak enough Spanish to translate that?" Rob asked. Blank faces greeted him.

He cued his radio. "Shane, you got ears on? Over." On the third try, Shane's dark voice replied.

"We're unloading the grocery stock and headed back for the rest before scavengers get to it. What's up? Over."

"How much Spanish do you remember from high school? Over."

"I'm fluent. Over."

"Can you get over here to Maggie's. Leave someone else to unload the truck. We need a translator. Over."

"Ten-four. Over and out."

"There going to be any trouble between you and Shane?" Jacob asked Jason directly.

"I think we settled it the other day, but I'll leave if it would be better. Maggie, I'll have someone stop back, make sure the genny's got gas. You get down to the shelter if you hear those sirens." Jason signaled his two guys and they left. Shane might have passed them in the parking lot, but Jacob didn't ask. The news broadcast had moved on by the time he got there.

"It's CNN Mexico, so they'll come back to the same news items soon," Shane announced without being asked. "Maggie, can I get something to eat?"

Maggie had been pretty once and she remained handsome enough, a big-breasted bleach- blonde whose face bore the stamp of a smoker. She had a robust voice with a sexy timbre.

"The kitchen's closed, but I have some microwave sandwiches. You want something to drink with that?"

"Coffee."

"Don't let your dad intimidate you," she said. *He's never been intimated by Rob, woman!* Shane laughed, shaking his head.

"I have way too much going on today for beer, but thanks. Maybe closer to sunset."

"You look tired," Jacob remarked as Maggie headed off to fill Shane's order. Shane smiled and nodded, leaning over the bar to pour a cup of coffee for himself.

"Sleeping in the front seat of my Jeep didn't really favor REM. So, just to get this out in the sunlight –I know about Cai and Marnie and I'm okay with it. I don't intend to have this conversation with anyone else, so if you will tell them all to back off and let me catch up to reality, I'd appreciate it."

223

"I guess we should have told you before you got here."

"Not you. You can't really put that in a text. Mom, though ... or Cai. They both emailed me. And, if the world hadn't blown up last night, I'd probably be mad, but what's the point now?"

That's what I thought he'd say.

"So, how do you intend to handle it?" Jacob asked aloud.

"I plan to pretend that Marnie is just some woman my brother married and walk away from her when she forgets."

"Sounds like the mature way to handle it." Because, really, how do you handle it any other way?

Jacob was about to say that when Shane turned to listen to the television.

"You follow soccer?" Jacob asked since it was clearly a sports segment and he could guess from the graphic that it was soccer.

"Cruz Azul is a friend's favorite *fotbal* team," Shane remarked, which answered Jacob's question and created a bunch more that went unasked.

Maggie brought the sandwich with a side of cheese, chips and a pickle. She liked Shane far more than she liked her new son-in-law. *How are you going to handle her, kid?* Shane thanked her and tucked in. He'd consumed the sandwich and was on his second cup of coffee when the top of the hour came around.

"Big story is the terrorist attacks in United States," Shane translated in a voice loud enough for anyone in the building to hear. "At least fifteen cities ... uh ... bombs ... fissionable material ...."

"Nuclear," Marvin Grosclose, the high school science teacher, said.

Shane was a good interpreter. He clearly knew the language well and had no trouble keeping up. Among the fifteen cities, the Mexicans worried about San Diego, Houston and Phoenix because of their proximity to the border. The US president and vice president were presumed dead along with a large percentage of Congress, all killed in Washington DC. The US diplomatic officials in Mexico claimed to have contact with US State Department personnel, but the state governments of Alaska and Hawaii had not heard from federal officials as yet. The person who took the Chicago skyline video had not been heard from since it was sent, but other Mexicans heard from families living in Texas. The UN made a statement calling for humanitarian aid and international justice. Financial markets were in turmoil and many governments were taking steps to stabilize their situations.

One of the teachers from the school took notes. Jacob didn't remember her name, but she'd been Keri's bridesmaid. *Odd name –Waltz, Rumba ...? Teacher at the school. Blasted old age!*

When the broadcast was done, they left the television running in case there was additional news as Rob, Bart, the fire chief Nathan Frear, and Jacob gathered around Shane.

"We need more information than Mexican news can give us," Rob began, then frowned when Anders McAuliff came up to his elbow.

"I know I'm not on the city management team, but I am chair of the city council and hosting one of the emergency shelters. Mind if I sit in?"

Rob nodded, but Jacob could see him willing himself not to glance toward Shane. Anders held out his hand toward the boy.

"I'm Anders McAuliff. I don't think we've met."

"Shane Delaney." The lift of his chin said Shane recognized the last name, but he shook hands anyway.

"Yeah." They met eyes briefly. Anders smiled like he meant it. "Don't worry about it. Let's deal with the crisis at hand. We need information. What about Topeka? Or Wichita?"

Rob spent the morning on the telephone, mostly talking to voice-mail. He knew the National Guard had closed the interstate, but he hadn't heard if it was open. When Shane reported what he and Cai had seen that morning, it became clear the interstate was not a good choice. Shane knew all sorts of routes to Topeka, though, thanks to his stint with Jason's trucking company.

"I could take the Stinson up, reconnoiter the route for you," Jacob offered. "Or fly you there."

"Aircraft aren't grounded?" Anders asked.

"The GA pilots in the air say there's been no such order."

The teacher glided up to join their group. Jacob truly admired sporty girls. This one moved like a graceful athlete.

"I tried to catch the cities on the news. It looks like there are sixteen confirmed," she told no one in particular. "Except for New York and Seattle, there aren't many big cities left."

"You've got to wonder why," Anders murmured. Shane admired Jazz without being overt about it, but now his gaze flicked toward Anders.

The door opened to admit five men. Jacob didn't like the scowl on Stan Osimowicz's face. "Rob."

"Stan, what brings you back this way?"

Shane and Paul eyed each other like two dogs about to fight over pack supremacy.

What's got your Irish up, Shane?

"Your boy stole a grocery shipment at gun point," Stan announced. Taller than Rob, who was a tall man, he kept his dark beard trimmed close and preferred cowboy boots over work boots.

"Is that the story he's telling?" Shane scoffed while he sized up the Mara Wells posse.

"Best to keep silence," Jacob warned softly, while worrying that Rob would act like Rob always had before.

"Let's us four go aside so we can speak privately."

Since he wasn't invited, Jacob turned to the young teacher.

"Jazz, right?"

"Yes. I feel like a third wheel with nothing to do. Could someone please assign me a task before I go crazy?"

"Now, you're talking. Your place ready for the fallout?"

"Fallout? What fallout?"

"Where do you live?"

"The apartments above Nick's."

"Nick isn't getting the building ready?"

"Nick was out of town. The last I heard, we were asked to stay calm and in our apartments, but I clearly can't follow instructions. There's probably 30 people who live in that building. What are we supposed to be doing?"

"Actually, providing shelter for people who won't fit into the other shelters, I think. Let's go take a look. That's if you got a car." She nodded and headed for the door. "Maggie, tell them I'm walking out with a gorgeous young lady."

Maggie saluted with her cigarette and Jacob followed Jazz out the door.

Collaboration

Emmaus

S hane Delaney hadn't served in the military, but he'd been to war. Stan could see it with the way he stood, aware of the entrances and any activity beyond the windows, while never taking his eyes off Paul. Stan remembered him as a wild kid, driving too fast and wrestling Paul in high school. Shane wore a loose shirt over a t-shirt (the better to hide his gun) and his jeans were soaked in dried blood. *Paul was wise to be afraid of you.*

"Shane, you want to tell me what this is all about?" Rob asked.

"Jos and I were at the train offloading Mae's shipment when Paul and some others showed up for their Cosco shipment. For some reason, Paul thought he could take Mae's shipment too."

"You know that's not true," Paul argued. "The Cosco shipment was already gone, because you took it!"

Shane's smooth forehead crinkled slightly.

"We only opened the one train car and I saw them taking things out of the others. I assumed it was the Cosco shipment, but I didn't verify it."

"You had all morning to clean those cars out," Paul countered.

"No, actually, he hasn't," Rob interjected. "He had just about enough time to get one truckload full of goods. And Jos can confirm it because he was with him."

"Where's Jos now?" Stan asked. Paul looked to the left and Shane stared at him. "Unloading Mae's shipment. I detailed a crew to go back to clean out the train, figuring to pick up whatever else beside the Cosco shipment was there."

Shane met Rob's gaze now.

"Good idea," Rob said. "Was it within the township?"

"Yes."

"Stan, I don't know where your shipment went, but Shane didn't have time to steal it. He was with Cai all night and then his time was accounted for all this morning."

Paul glared at Shane. After all these years, Frank had established himself as a trustworthy worker and he was busy resupplying the diesel. It was just food missing and Shane wasn't lying. Paul, however....

"I believe you," Stan said. Paul gave him an astounded glance. "I'll verify with Jos, of course. Mind if I detail a crew to the train as well?"

"We can take turns," Rob agreed. "Shane, make sure our crew keeps an eye out for the Cosco shipment and they don't touch it."

"Yes, sir."

Neither of you is lying. What's going on here?

"Sounds good. Shane, nice you made it home for this."

Shane snorted and smiled, though it didn't actually make it to his eyes.

"Yeah. I have *great* timing." Then he looked toward the television. Rob glanced at him as he strode closer.

"What is it?" Stan asked.

"I don't speak Spanish, but he does. He'll start translating in a minute."

"The Department of Homeland Security spoke with CNN Mexico, asking them to spread the word that people need to prepare bomb shelters. DHS will be contacting local and regional governments as soon as possible." A graphic appeared on the screen--North America with cloud cover, but also some strange swirls that Stan had not seen before. "Rain is forecast for this area. In the evening. DHS recommends we harvest as soon as radiation levels drop and that we butcher any animals we can't get into a protected shelter. Now they're describing the sort of shelter we need to survive this thing."

"We already know that," Rob noted.

"We're going to head to Mara to keep things rolling," Stan announced. "I'm sorry for this unpleasantness, Rob. Your boy's reputation precedes itself   "

"It had to have been him, Dad!"

"But it couldn't have been," Stan snapped. "We'll figure it out. We don't have time for this right now. Rob, if our Geigers pick up elevated rads, we'll use the storm alarms to warn people. Your folks that way should hear it."

Shane turned from the television.

"Dad, I'm going to make sure Alex knows that. Most the folks out that way are deaf. He's going to have to figure out some way to get the word out."

By the time Stan Osimowicz and his crew said their pleasantries to Rob and Maggie, Shane's Jeep was already gone from the parking lot.

"Dad, you're believing that lying sack of --."

"I'm believing Rob, yes. Somebody else could have gotten to that shipment first. Let's swing over to the grocery store and see what Jos has to say before we head for the barn."

You're the one lying, kid, but I don't have time to deal with it now. Radiation will get us before hunger.

Being Poppy

Emmaus

*S*orm barn underground. Cows goats protected except roof but cover with dirt. All good. Piling bales against walls of barn, across the mow. Micah, Joel bringing their cows, chickens, pigs. Pete good worker, not know much. Doesn't stop. Phone dead charging. Can't talk. Hate this.

Sky pretty bright blue smell of lightning to west. Swallow, feel ears pop slight. Hour? Two?

Poppy tapped Keri on the shoulder and told her. Keri nodded, but didn't pause from leading the horses into the storm barn even as Alex operated the backhoe to cover the metal roof with compost. Poppy continued with taking water to Pete in the barn where he stacked hay bales.

Parents at grocery store, helping there. Where stay during rain? Maybe here?

Pete gratefully took the water bottle, poured some over his head and drank about half in three gulps. He asked her a question, but his sign was still rudimentary, and she couldn't read speech that well. He finger-spelled "rain."

She provided the sign for "rain", then pointed to the clock above the tool bench and showed one

233

hour -- two hour. He frowned. She signed "parents".
He looked baffled.

"Parents," she said aloud. He shrugged. *So
frustrating!*

They worked for about twenty minutes in
silence, closing up the gaps.

*Cousins here with trucks. Unload animals.
Mocha bring goats.*

She gestured for Pete to come help with getting
Alex's herds into the storm barn. The heat and
humidity stuck her hair to her neck and forehead.

A green Jeep pulled up the long driveway and a
man got out. He looked familiar, but it wasn't until
he signed her name that she recognized him.
Shane! He looked so different with his hair cut
short and she'd grown so he didn't seem so tall
anymore.

"You how you?"

"Fine. Alex?" His signing was rusty, slow.

Alex saw him and pushed his way through
goats and cows to get to him. Shane spoke and Alex
interpreted.

"Rob say you need warn your people tornado
sirens sound. Go to shelters."

*"Know that you. Hearing dogs there, there, there,
all over. Rain smell coming. Know that.*

Shelters finished soon. You go home? Or ...?"
"Jason Breen – warn – concrete buildings."

Shane and Alex looked up as a helicopter flew
overhead. Poppy recognized it as Ren Sullivan's
helicopter. Alex signed *"Wichita? Now? Weird."* Then
he realized she was still standing there. *"You back
to work you."*

Poppy moved off, but slowly, glancing over her
shoulder. Alex stopped signing, so Poppy didn't
know what they said, but their expressions were
grave. Then Keri told her and Pete to transport

bedding and food into the storm shelter and she
didn't have time to wonder anymore.

Home Sweet Bomb Shelter

Jericho West of Emmaus

*W*hat *to tell and when to tell it?*
He'd promised he would, and he intended
to, but maybe not all of it. Grant had lived
with secrets for so long, he wasn't sure he could
give them all up in a day.

He'd already told them most of it on Tuesday
night when they'd finally pulled into the driveway.
They'd slept in the motor homes that night and
spent most of yesterday bringing things into the 15-
room house. When the CSA had bought it from
Sullivan, they'd left most of the rooms intact to
maintain the illusion of a bed and breakfast. The
basement, however, was a different story.

Two years' worth of food and medicine and a
small armory took up fully half of the ordinary
basement, but the area under the garage was a
fully concrete-enclosed bomb shelter behind a
heavy door. One of the four rooms had a small
stash of survival supplies arranged neatly on floor
to ceiling shelves. There was a bunk room, a battery
bank with a generator and a common room filled
with a bank of servers and a table with several
hardened laptops,

They stared around, looking pale. It might have just been the LED light or maybe they were truly stunned. How that was possible after Grant and Dylan had told them about the terrorist plot and it had actually happened ... people loved to cling to normality even when it was clear that it was no longer possible.

"The weather report says the rain will hit before sundown. We need to get into the shelter."

"Will it be enough?" Jim asked.

"It will. The walls are concrete. The roof is the concrete floor of the garage. We have a water tank, fuel and it's only for a few days. I've already set the outside sensors, so we'll know when to come out."

"What about the people in that town?" Madalyn asked.

"I can't help them any more than I could help the people who died yesterday."

"I can't believe you're saying that," Emily said. Mother and daughter were clear -- they believed he should have waved a red flag. Emily would forgive him eventually, but Madalyn ... it was going to be a long winter, for Jim as well as for him.

"We really don't have time to discuss this," Jim announced. "Let's get ourselves arranged, make sure we have everything we need down here. We'll have time to discuss all of this later, but we have to live through the next few days."

He began giving them each an assignment, taking charge in a way Grant had not expected. Jim stunned Grant by giving him a job, but he didn't argue, didn't want to set anyone else against obeying.

There were three bunk beds for eight people, but the couch folded out into a double bunk, which the women announced Grant and Dylan could sleep on. Jim didn't try to talk them out of it. Dylan followed Grant upstairs to gather more blankets because they could already tell the shelter was chronically cool. He filled his pockets with two decks of cards that existed for the sham of this being a bed and breakfast.

"So, when do we start to do something about this?" he asked as they stripped one of the beds.

"I don't know. My goal is to assure our survival and then …. The equipment works, but it's not something we can do when they're in the shelter with us."

"Why not, Dad?" Dylan demanded. "If this is the life we lead from now on … why shouldn't they know what we know?"

He gathered up an armload of blankets and walked away, leaving Grant with a lot to think about.

Into the Fire

Emmaus

Jason Breen felt a hand on his shoulder and looked from the drill bit to see a green Jeep pulling into the compound. The sky to the west took on an increasing shade of green-blue suggesting rain and he knew what that meant. He set the drill down.

"Keep hanging the plywood," he told Gene and walked toward Shane. "You are either the bravest bastard that's ever lived or you really think highly of my honor."

"Or I don't care if you kill me." He almost smiled. He wore a ball cap over his short hair and took off his sunglasses so Jason could see his eyes. He nodded to the truckers enclosing the windows of the only concrete-roofed structure in the complex. "Looks like you already know what's coming."

"Local radio works." Out of the corner of his eye, Jason saw the hay field across the interstate bow toward the east. "If we have forty minutes, I'll be surprised."

"Is that a concrete roof?"

"Yup."

"Then I'm headed on. Before I go -- I didn't mean for Josh to get caught up in that."

241

Lela Markham

"I know. Not saying I forgive you, but that I know it wasn't deliberate. Sometime when we're not about to fry, you'll have to explain how it went down. Do you know about Marnie and ...?"

Shane's gaze shifted behind him and now Jason heard it too, the clank and chatter of metal. He looked behind him and saw a convoy of military vehicles racing down the Interstate toward Denver.

"What the hell?"

They stood there staring at the strangest parade Jason had ever seen -- APCs, tanks, a couple of trailers with backhoes and other gear. Shane broke first.

"Yeah, I know about them. Got to go."

"Any idea where the Army's going?"

"To die, I would guess," Shane replied as a gust of wind brought a scent of rain to them. "They're going to fry in those tin cans."

He got into his car and drove away. Jason turned back to his men.

"Pick up the pace. Rain's coming."

Going to Ground

Emmaus

Rob pointed to Glister's bed and told the dog "Down, stay." Belle the cat hissed from her carrier. Jill set down the box of food in the corner near the cots.

The radio crackled then Cai's voice came on.

"We're closing up the Medical Center. We're out of room."

"Everything under control?"

"Bas ran a maintenance check. I guess we are as good as we can be for a room that's been excess storage for forty years. Shane with you guys?"

"No, we're not sure where he is."

"He can take care of himself, Dad. Don't worry on that score. Last night he was a hero and officially became the scariest person I know."

"Yeah, we'll all have to talk about what he's been doing for the last few years ... after the rain."

"I think I know what he's been doing, but he'd probably be pissed if we talked about it on an open radio channel."

"Good thought. Stay safe. City Hall has the monitors, so they'll let us know when the radiation levels drop back to the safety margin."

Bart Rawlson keyed in.

"I just heard the Mara Wells sirens," he announced. "Just getting things tied up here on the roof while Bob cranks the sirens."

"Good, Bart. My house phone is ringing." Jill ducked through the door to get it. "We may lose radio communications once this hits so just sit tight until the rad levels go down and then hit the sirens again to let us know."

"Got it," Bart assured.

Rob set the radio down and joined Jill at the phone. "It's Stan Osimowicz."

"Rob, I couldn't get anyone at City Hall. The radiation levels are starting to climb, so we're locking it down. See you on the far side of this."

"Yes."

"I just want to apologize for that unpleasantness this afternoon and hope it won't affect our working together."

"It won't. Shane's reputation precedes him. It's a bit mistaken, but I can understand where people wonder."

"Good to know. See you on the far side then."

They hung up. Rob stared around the basement, hearing a roll of far-off thunder. Jill waited in the shelter.

"I guess we won't have to worry about Shane teasing us about that time," she said.

"No, but I'm sure he's fine. He was headed to Alex's."

"Right and he thought he'd have to spend this time with Cai and Marnie, so he was probably being sensible."

"Right." Thunder rolled again. "Time to close it up," Rob decided. "We'll deal with everything else after the rain."

In Concrete We Trust

Emmaus

One of Emmaus's business blocks started life as an airplane factory during the Depression. Closed in the 1970s industrial crash, it had been converted to retail and apartment space since. A long-unused corridor connected the two ends, separated from the old production bay by a concrete wall. It neatly held the forty people Jacob was entrusted with.

"What was this space back in the day?" Jazz asked Jacob as they set up a honey bucket in the abandoned bathroom. It appeared the old sewer drain was open. They were testing the theory with a hose.

"The production bay was noisy. The concrete blocked the sound for this area of employee lockers and a break room where Nick's shops are. When the aircraft company closed, Ren's dad bought the building for a song and asked me to come in as a 10% partner. I remodeled the street fronts for shops, but this concrete wall was in my way here, so I left this side for later, then never got to it. The production bay was always enough for storage for the entire block, even when my feed shipments are overflowing. Ren built the apartments but sold to

245

Lela Markham

me and Nick when he couldn't rent them for as much as he thought they were worth."

If Jazz thought he rambled like an old man, she didn't say anything. She just got back to the subject at hand.

"So, the walls of my apartment are concrete and so is the roof and floor, which means we're protected on all sides?"

"Except for the doors, but feed sacks and bags of flour are mass, so we should be fine."

"Yeah, through the rain. What happens after?"

Jacob estimated the hose had gone into the drain twenty feet. That should be enough for now. "Good question. Life as we knew it is over. After we're done trusting our safety to concrete, we'll have to learn to use our heads again. Not sure folks know that yet, but that's what's coming."

Jacob saw the hairs on her arm stand up and she shivered.

"The fundamental transformation of the United States?" she suggested.

"I'm hoping we're not some sort of sociological experiment, but it sure feels like someone threw a catalyst into our petrie dish, doesn't it?"

"Yeah. And I am so worried about my mom and dad and brothers. Is everybody you care about trusting to concrete?"

"I don't know about my daughters. Ada lives in Seattle, which Shane said they didn't hit, and Inez lives Germany, so she's probably okay. Everybody else – well, we haven't heard from Shane since he headed to Alex's, but if anyone can take care of themselves, it's probably him."

"He's interesting," Jazz said.

Jacob smiled at her. *Maybe a part of helping Shane involves a good woman.*

"He is, if you don't want life to be too tame."

246

"I don't think life is going to be that for a while."

Thunder vibrated through the concrete walls. Several children began to bawl.

"I think we've done what we can in here," Jacob announced, coiling up the hose. "Nothing to do now but keep folks calm and think of a lot of road trip games."

"I was really good at those when I was a kid."

"Good. You get the first shift then. Make it a hard one so I can have some time to think about mine."

"Yes, sir!"

In the corridor a couple of men finished placing feed bags against one of the door walls. A line of mattresses, hastily pulled from the apartments lined one wall, food and water lined the other, leaving a narrow walkway. Another roll of thunder ramped up the tension in the room.

"Hey, let's play a game," Jazz said loudly. "It's called a yes-no mystery. You can ask me yes or no questions and you use my yes or no answers to solve the mystery."

Distracted by events, the kids seemed only mildly interested, but Jacob remembered these. Shane and Cai spent hours trying to get the answer out of Rob.

"There's a cabin in the woods. Everyone inside is dead. What happened?"

Jacob sat down on the cot he'd dragged in from the feed store and idling listened while Jazz tried to distract from the storm outside.

God, I've got no real reason to worry. Shane's a resourceful kid, but .... Keep your eye on him, Lord, and put him in the place You need him to be.

One Misstep

Jericho Springs

S hane hadn't planned to go to Jericho Springs, but when he paused at Lufgren's Crossing he saw tire tracks on the road. Two vehicles larger than his Jeep had come by here since he'd been to the hotel. He turned and drove north, watching the fast-moving cumulus spilling over the ridge to his left.

Seeing two motor homes in the yard of the Sullivan place surprised him. Whoever they were, they had the keys to the gate. Shane pulled up beside them and knocked on the front door. Nobody answered. He tried to look through the shutters, but they were all closed and locked. He remembered Jacob telling him that the Sullivans built a bomb shelter under the garage in the 1950s. He decided to check back after he checked the well. After all, if they survived the next few days, that well would keep them alive through the winter.

Jusilla's Creek ran full of water and grass, which he had not seen in his lifetime. He drove over the bridge, parked near the hotel and strode up the hill to the blue-and-white concrete building that the well pumps rested in. Actually, they weren't' pumps, they were valves, meant to control the artesian well. There was a large tank on the hill behind the building, meant to hold an emergency reservoir. Water poured out of a port on the side. He needed to get that closed before it destabilized the hill.

Wind tugging at his clothes, Shane climbed to the roof, then up a ladder on the side of the tank. It was an emergency relief port for when the tank was over-full. From this vantage point he could see that the overflow hose lay on the ground beneath the tank, a victim of pressure it probably hadn't been rated for. Shane heard the tornado siren sound far to the west. He started down the ladder. Thunder rolled, sounding like mortar fire. He had to go, worry about the well later. He turned as thunder rolled again. A dark robbed figure moved near the hotel. He felt the AR in his hand and swiveled toward her. His foot came down in the inch deep-water flowing across the path into the creek. Mud oozed. His foot slid sideways. He hit the ground hard on one shoulder, slid and tumbled and slammed face first into the bottom of the creek.

"And what rough beast, its hour come round at last, slouches toward Bethlehem to be born?
William Butler Yeats

###

The End

Excerpt from Objects in View

Emmaus

Life ticked away one breath at a time as one by one they yawned and found a place to rest on the floor, backs to the walls, heads in each other's laps or upon each other's shoulders.

They thought they just settled down to sleep, to wait out the toxic rain and then face what had become of their world fully rested. They didn't sense their ensuing doom. Occasionally someone protested that it was stuffy or hot, but few others were awake to hear them.

The hours ticked by and soon all slept. Nobody noticed the mouse curled in the corner, breathing its last. The people died more slowly, smothered by the lack of oxygen and the increasing carbon dioxide level. Bart Rawlson suffered convulsions causing his wife to open her eyes briefly, but when he stopped jerking, she soon closed her eyes and sank closer to death.

They'd worried about the radiation, not the ventilation. Modern man lost the little things that modern man in his technological advance and that would spell their deaths in this new world. They knew how to set up a remote sensor to monitor the radiation levels, but not how to check a belt to assure it was still processing air.

Jacob and Jazz went from person to person, checking pulses. They found some clinging to life -- several children, young women, teenage boys -- those with more efficient breathing, stronger hearts. Once carried out into the fresh air, they began to revive. They were the lucky ones. Over seventy-five people suffocated. They wouldn't be the last to die, Jacob knew. They might not even be the first. How many people were missed and died in the radiation storm? Not that trusting to concrete seemed much better for the folks at City Hall. Jacob watched as men from the school shelter, pressed into service, carried the bodies out. He watched dry-eyed and wished he thought ahead and saved his friends but wishing wouldn't make it so. He'd seen battle like this in the past, once that had gone wrong. You had to analyze them, grieve for those who didn't make it, accept what could not be changed and move on. Like war, he doubted they'd have time for the grieving part. Dealing with the central situation of nuclear apocalypse would likely grab most of that attention.

Jazz didn't weep either at first, until they carried out Marv Groseclose and then she turned aside to puke in a storm drain. Jacob held her while she wept, fighting back his own tears for Bart, when Rob and Jill arrived. Jill went immediately to help care for those who could be saved.

"Where's Marnie and Cai?" Rob demanded with rigid control. "And has anyone seen Shane?"

Stay Tuned for the Rest of the Story

☐

Other Great Books

Moscow, 2138. With the world only beginning to recover from the complete societal collapse of the late 21st Century, Zoya scrapes by prepping corpses for funerals and dreams of saving enough money to have a child. When her brother forces her to bring him a mysterious package, she witnesses his murder and finds herself on the run from ruthless mobsters. Frantically trying to stay alive and save her loved ones, Zoya opens the package and discovers two unusual data cards, one that allows her to fight back against the mafia and another which may hold the key to everlasting life.

The Immorality Game by Ted Cross

Books by Lela Markham

Transformation Project by Lela Markham

Daermad Cycle by Lela Markham

Meet Lela Markham

Hi. I was raised in a house made of books in Alaska and told tales from the time I could talk. A teacher eventually made me write one of them down. I hated the exercise, but it was the spark that ignited a fire that has never gone out.

My daring husband, two fearless offspring and I live the adventure of a lifetime here on the Last Frontier where the midnight sun encourages wandering the wilderness and the long dark winters favor reading, writing and staring at the northern lights … hence the moniker Aurorawatcher.

It's all about the aurora watching!